Lakeside
Imagination

VOLUME 1

Lakeside
Imagination

Unemployed Idealist

Lakeside Imagination: Volume 1

Printed in the United States of America
ISBN 978-1-64133-807-3 (hc)
ISBN 978-1-64133-805-9 (sc)
ISBN 978-1-64133-806-6 (e)

2024.04.01

This book is printed on acid-free paper.

BlueInk Media Solutions
1111B S Governors Ave
STE 7582 Dover,
DE 19904

www.blueinkmediasolutions.com

Introduction

I have a confession to make. I have never really enjoyed sermons. It isn't for lack of trying. I took notes, drew outlines, looked up verses, cross-referenced passages, and generally acted interested in every way I knew how, all to little avail. Now, I believe that listening to something good for you out of a sense of duty won't hurt a person. But when life put me in a place where I was expected to share sermons, I wasn't willing to be listened to out of a sense of duty, even if I stumbled upon an audience prepared to do that.

When we started a Sunday service at the campground on the lake where my family lives, I purposed to find a way to share a message that would depend not on a sense of duty in the audience but on a sense of the fullness and beauty of the lake, and the woods surrounding us. That ushered in a Renaissance of storytelling in my world. I had always loved stories, so I began to craft stories that would both engage an audience and share a message. Many of the plots I borrowed from the parables in the Bible, but the characters were patterned after people I knew, who lived in places where I have been.

The first story in this book is the first story I told instead of a sermon. As I continued to share these stories, I found many others who welcomed my message in the form of a story. Weekly, I go to our local jail and tell stories such as these to individuals who often find themselves enjoying an interesting story, only to be surprised by a message that hits home.

After telling these stories many times for many different audiences, I would occasionally be asked to write one down for a particular person. Sometimes, I would find the time to fulfill such a request, and gradually, the number of stories in written form grew. Those who enjoyed them in both oral and written form have often encouraged me to create what you hold in your hand, a collection of stories meant to entertain and encourage you along your life's journey.

For those of you passionate about grammar and punctuation, let me offer this warning. Where possible (with the help of friends), I have conformed to the rules; however, stylistically, I was guided not by published standards but by how they sounded. These stories began in the oral tradition, and it is my hope that they will often be passed on orally to others. When you think of a friend who might like a story, I encourage you to read it to them, allowing them to listen with their ears and hopefully with their heart. Punctuation is used carefully but sometimes creatively, more to make the story readable than to please an English teacher.

With all that being said, I hope that you enjoy these stories and that they bring you closer to one who long ago sat with friends and neighbors on the shores of Lake Genessaret and prompted them to imagine a Kingdom not of this world.

Jeremy Davies
22511 Long Lake Dr.
Shevlin MN 56676
northwoods.jeremy@hotmail.com

Table of Contents

Home Again

Before farms in this country were dignified (or slandered) with the title "agri-business," they were categorized as part of our infrastructure. Like roads, trains, and power lines, they were a part of the countryside we needed to conduct our lives. Willard Teply still ran that style of farm. He knew it might be fiscally advantageous to specialize, but he continued to raise pigs, milk cows, make hay, grow grain, and even keep enough chickens to sell eggs. Most of the neighbors had begun raising exclusively grain, but Willard's grandfather had farmed this land. Willard wouldn't feel right about calling something a farm having no four-legged or feathered inhabitants.

Despite his resistance to progressive ideas and his clear disregard for the sensibilities of "the experts," his farm made money. Since he had formally taken over the farm from his father, he had purchased two neighboring farms. Yet, what made that purchase and his whole farm unusual was the fact that he had paid cash for both. Everything on the farm was paid in full, and every account was fully settled at the end of each month.

Ownership was intertwined with stewardship in Willard's mind. The farm was completely his, but he held it with a view to his sons.

Willard and his wife, Rose, had two boys, Toby and Rick. They were just under a year apart, but because of their specific dates of birth, they were both in the same grade at school. Toby was older and usually understood that being a grade ahead of his brother wouldn't have been that much better, but sometimes, he resented not getting as many of the privileges an "older brother" should get. Willard and Rose were sensitive to this, and there were some dates that went without any chance of compromise. No matter how much Rick hinted and begged, he didn't get his first pocket knife until he was six years old, just like Toby. During deer hunting season, Rick wasn't even allowed to come along and watch until he was fully licensed. But the parents also recognized that most of the advantages due to someone eleven months, two weeks, and six days older than his sibling were imagined. Their concern was that Toby would develop the sensitivities of a victim towards the perceived injustice of not being treated as older, so they emphasized to each of the boys the advantages of having a friend who was always there to join you and consistently pointed out the complimentary aspect of their personalities.

Anyone who observed the boys closely was sure to notice how they differed. Both were bright, but Toby was a builder, and Rick was a dreamer. Toby wanted things to pile up like bricks— one completely formed idea upon another. He always had the patience to finish step one before he began step two and a vision for the details that might not affect step one but would definitely undermine step two. From the heights at which Rick's imagination soared, it was difficult even to focus on the details that so often consumed his brother's attention. Ideas filled his head, consumed his attention briefly, and passed on with little care to their usefulness or practicality.

The relationship between the boys was greatly improved by their good fortune of growing up on a farm. A farm with the variety of activities found on the Teply farm had "real work" for the boys, almost from the time they could put on their own manure boots. The boys quickly found that by working together, they could accomplish far more than they could alone. The division of labor between them became almost automatic. Rick would invent labor-saving devices, and Toby would provide the labor. Toby was large enough to dissuade Rick (sometimes forcefully) from trying to boss him around, and Rick's ideas were often successful enough for Toby to be inclined to grant him leeway in investing some of his time in his latest scheme.

By the time they were young men, the boys were inseparable. They had become a mainstay of the labor at the farm and, each year, were given more work and, along with it, more responsibility. Away from the farm, they were impressing people too. Constant physical labor hardened the boys' muscles and trained their coordination so that their natural athletic abilities were honed to a fine edge. In the fall, Toby, at quarterback, always seemed to be able to connect with Rick, and their football team set the state nine-man football record for passing yards gained. Their partnership continued on the basketball court and the baseball diamond where, in the spring, Rick pitched and Toby caught.

Academically, the boys did well, and although they occasionally participated in some of the unapproved extracurricular activities to which they were constantly invited as heroes of the local sports team, they "stayed out of trouble."

Staying out of trouble seemed to be the standard to which they were called. Had the boys had a maturity that comes with age, they could have seen that their father had no greater concern than preparing them for their future. His decisions were constantly guided by how to run the farm so that his sons would desire to join him someday, but he knew that they must be drawn to such a choice, not driven. He required enough work from them to produce young men of discipline, but beyond that, he gave them great leeway to make choices for themselves. He imposed upon himself, countering his desire to manage things, an attitude of interest and encouragement towards his sons' choices.

No parent, though, desires to have their children make mistakes, even if they can learn from them, so Willard and Rose tried to carefully warn their sons about the pitfalls they should avoid. To the ears of the boys at their age and development, the result was that it seemed that their parents' cherished ambition was that they "stay out of trouble." To the boys, the lists of things they shouldn't do seemed to be much more clearly elucidated than any positive ambitions for their lives. Don't do this. Don't do that. Don't hang out with this kind of person. Don't go to those places. This seemed to be the most important message they received; however, they weren't interested in most of the things they were being advised against. The result was that the warnings and prohibitions actually served to whet an appetite for the activities their parents wanted to steer them away from. A person might warn you, "Don't eat dirt." You would say, "Fine, I don't want to." But if they continued to warn you, it could very easily trigger an interest in finding out why someone would want to eat dirt.

Toby and Rick loved their lives on the farm and had little interest in cultivating many outside interests. Both felt that one of the negative aspects of their athletic prowess was that it kept them away from home for too many hours. The farm was where they loved to be, and whether it was working on a project in the shop or walking in the woods that bordered the pasture, the activities were unquestionably wholesome. But as the warning against the pitfalls of normal teenage life continued, a question began to hover in the boys' consciousness. "Am I missing something?"

They were in the middle of their senior year when Willard planned a special weekend for them. He rented a very comfortable ice house on Lake of the Woods so that they could spend time together just hanging out. He planned a mixture of fishing, watching some movies, and talking, without the pressures of the normal farm chores. The fact that Willard had arranged for someone to look after the farm let the boys know that this was of comparable importance to a funeral or a wedding.

As they spent time together, Willard led the conversation to the future. He shared with the boys some of the business decisions he had made and how they were intended to make staying on the farm a viable option for them. "I don't want to lock you into something you don't want to do, but I want you to know that I would be honored to have you officially join me on the farm. I know your interests may differ, but we have a lot of freedom to move the farm in another direction that might fit better with your interests.

"I love you both, and I'm proud of you. I want you to follow your dreams. Maybe there is some way we can do that together," he concluded.

The boys were touched by the clear affirmation. Though they never doubted their father's support, he was typically less verbal about his emotions.

Rick spoke up first. "Dad, I love the farm, but I want to get out into the world. I want to go to college."

"I was hoping you would want to. Any idea where?"

"California," Rick replied confidently.

"Are you sure? It would be a lot more affordable to stay in state. It would be easier to get home to visit too."

"Dad, I don't want it to be easy to get home. I want to go somewhere where I can live a totally different life. I know what it's like to live in a small community in Minnesota. But I want to see what it's like to go somewhere different and meet different people and try different things." Willard resisted the urge to insist on something more practical. He understood that these were Rick's dreams, not his, and he knew that even if he could keep him close for a little while longer, this son would never be satisfied until he had gotten away.

Toby remained quiet, so Willard prompted him. "What are your plans?"

"I don't know...I guess I'll stay and help you on the farm. I've never really thought about anything else."

Through springtime, the plans were gradually solidified. Willard began structuring the farm as a corporation so that Toby could become a legal partner when he graduated. The function of the farm wasn't affected much, but the paperwork had to be filed. Plus, it gave Toby a feeling of importance to be officially part of the process. Rick's plans also were coming together. He had settled on a private college in a smaller town north of Sacramento, California. It was academically respected and seemed to offer courses of study that would likely interest him; at least, that was the picture drawn by the copious material sent from the admissions department. The picture Rick got from his research on the Internet he kept to himself: it sounded like this was a party school, and the stories he read on one of the blogs made it sound like a pretty wild campus. Rick wanted to explore life, and this seemed to be the place.

Willard had the biggest challenge to his positive attitude when he was shown the price. It staggered him to think that they would charge the price of a new car just to teach a kid for a year. He tried to steer Rick to something more reasonable, but Rick had his heart set on this school. The material from the school emphasized the availability of student loans, but Willard balked at the idea of borrowing money for something as intangible as a liberal arts education. He finally one day sat down with Rick to talk.

"Rick, is this what you really want?"

"Yeah, Dad, this is what I want."

"I can't afford to send you to school there unless I do something to get the money. Do you remember three years ago when I bought the Olson farm?"

Rick nodded, "Uh-huh."

"I bought that land specifically so that you could farm it someday. But I used most of the money we had saved. That farm can produce enough to pay for an in-state public college. But, if you really want to go to a private school in California, I have found someone who will buy the land from me."

"Okay." And with hardly a thought, Rick traded a solid piece of this earth for the fleeting dream of something, if not better, then more appealing.

By late summer, everything was in place. Rick had his blue Pontiac Grand Am loaded with everything he thought he would need in his new life. Both parents thought it might be good to take him to college and had been planning the trip when Rick insisted that he wanted to go alone. Although he knew he would miss home, he was getting more excited every day about the new world to which he was headed. He didn't want his first impression to be colored by the opinions of Mom and Dad.

The land had been sold, and for tax purposes, the money was placed into a fund in Rick's name. The fund provided sufficient money to cover tuition, books, and housing, plus a monthly stipend for Rick's expenses. Despite the disappointment at having Rick seem so anxious to distance himself from his home and family, Willard wanted him to have every chance to be successful in his education.

Rick's first quarter in college was almost like a new birth for him. College life was the exact opposite of home life. It seemed like the goal of the college was to provide an environment where no discipline was necessary. Rick's earliest class was at 9:30 meaning he could sleep until about 9:20, three hours later than at home. And unlike home, where the sphere of contact was small, at school, there were always people to hang out with. Rick had an engaging personality, and he was pretty good-looking. Soon, he found himself on the regular circuit of parties. He also had money to spend, which is always a plus when it comes to buying the beverages essential to the parties.

By the second quarter, he had established himself as one of the necessary ingredients to any successful party. He had the personality and creativity to make a mundane party into something memorable, at least to anyone who was able to remember anything about the night. A circle of students emerged whose first question about any gathering was, "Will Rick be there?" As a result, he began to not just be invited but also recruited for parties, and the hosts could always count on him to make a financial contribution to the festivities.

The spring quarter marked a new step for Rick in his chosen career as a party animal. He was making active provisions for the lifestyle. A careful examination of the student handbook revealed a loophole in college policy. The minimum number of credits to remain a full-time student (the key to receiving Rick's full student stipend) could be reduced below the normal level if a class was dropped after the third week of class. However, cross-referencing the policy, he discovered that a partial refund would be credited to the student's personal account if the drop was taken before mid-term. This added boost to his income, coupled with a very light schedule of classes (none of which was scheduled earlier than 11:15 am), sufficed to make partying not just for weekends anymore.

His grades showed the results of this life, and his grades in Macroeconomics, while not reaching the failing point, were low enough that he would have to retake the course before enrolling in Microeconomics. Since Rick was beginning to think that a business major probably afforded him the best opportunity to get a high-paying degree, and since he didn't really want to go home and face his family, he wrote home asking if the funds could be made available to retake Macroeconomics during the summer quarter.

When he received an affirmative answer, he purposed to concentrate on his studies throughout the summer. He succeeded for the most part and passed the course with the necessary grade to proceed.

The fall quarter came, and with it, the bulk of the student body returned, many of whom, after a summer of work, were ready to get back to the social life of college. Rick, who felt like he had behaved himself pretty well through the summer, decided he needed a reward and plunged into the flurry of celebrations among returning friends. His summer, rather than getting him back on the right track, only served as the evidence he presented to his uneasy conscience that he didn't have a problem; he could still control things.

Rick's failure to return home hurt Toby. Even though his parents accepted at face value the reasons offered by their youngest son, what Toby read between the lines fit well with some of the unguarded stories Rick shared with him over the phone when Mom and Dad weren't on the line. Toby's hurt might have passed on or prompted him to break out of the patterns of life which were already beginning to hem him in had it not been for a seemingly innocuous comment made by one of Willard's friends. A nearby farmer had stopped by to visit on a rainy fall day. Willard and Toby were working in the shop, waiting out the rain, and enjoyed the social call. While they were standing around the pickup, they discussed many things: the weather, the crops, the prices, and the latest news from Rick. The conversation had progressed that far when Rose called to Willard from the house. It was a phone call for which he had been waiting, and he ran up to the house to answer it.

The conversation lagged until the farmer said to Toby, "I'll bet your Dad is grateful for the sacrifice you made staying home to help him. I know he counts on you a lot."

Toby liked the sound of that.

As he mulled it over that evening while he was milking the cows, he reviewed the last year in the light of the "sacrifice" comment. Here he was, giving up the chance to have fun just for the sake of the farm and his father. It was quite a sacrifice. He somehow forgot that the farm officially belonged, in part, to him and that he hadn't wanted to leave. What he had "given up" had never existed in his mind. But now, each time he thought about it, he would inflate the assessment of his forsaken potential in the hope that he would get a corresponding boost in the level of satisfaction he could feel about giving it up.

He cherished visitors coming to the farm because, now that he was attuned to sacrifice comments, Toby realized that they were by no means unusual. Often, when he would make an excuse to go inside the house, dirty with the honest dirt of hard labor, it would prompt comments from the guests sitting around the table visiting with Willard and Rose. He often left his gloves behind just for the satisfaction of returning to the sudden awkward but smiling silence, which meant they had been talking about him.

Rick, on the other hand, was finding little satisfaction in his life. His sophomore year was giving him little chance to break out of the role in which he had cast himself. The concerns and shame he felt began to induce him to like himself better drunk than sober. At least then, he could be a cheerful, outgoing person, and any irritating personality traits could be excused by the alcohol or by the fact that he was still getting enough money to bankroll much of the fun.

Gradually, he found more ways to access the funds in his account. One of the easiest was through the purchase of textbooks. By submitting the receipts for textbooks he needed, he could get a reimbursement check. His parents had no way of knowing that he had returned the books to the bookstore for a cash refund. He would buy used books, check them out from the library, or just ignore them if he thought he could pass the course without them.

He spent spring quarter on academic probation because of his grades and stayed again through the summer to try to catch up on the classes he would need to graduate. His grades didn't meet the technical requirements to get him off academic probation, but at least they were showing improvement. The Dean of Students chose to let him register for fall quarter with a very clear caveat: unless Rick gave up the partying and the alcohol, he doubted very much whether Rick had a chance of graduating. Rick promised that he would and really sincerely intended to. He did, in fact, for three weeks and four days, which seemed to him like a very long time, especially in light of being constantly invited by "friends" to join them for a night of fun.

Friday night of his fourth week, he thought he deserved a little break, but it ended up not being a little break. It was ten days before he could break away from the grip that the wild life had on him. He determined to quit the parties and the drinking but found himself caught on the roller coaster ride of binges and regrets. Somehow, he made the grades necessary to continue for another quarter, but shortly before it was time to register for the winter quarter, he received a statement of funds for his education account. It was nearly depleted. All his schemes for milking the account were catching up to him, and he realized that he barely had enough money left for the rest of his junior year. He didn't dare to face his father, not after all the lies he'd told. His courage was further diminished by the likelihood that his father would very justly refuse to give him anything more.

Well, he could always work his way through college.

Winter quarter, he registered for the maximum class load and purchased all the necessary books. Then, just before the start of classes, he quit school. He argued with himself that it wasn't really wrong to keep the refunded money since he would use it to get settled into an apartment and to find a job where he could save up the money to continue his education.

He found a decent job and a comfortable apartment. One of the big differences between college and a career is the wonderfully freeing sensation of being done at the end of each workday. In college, you always have papers or studying hanging over your head, but you give them the required hours at work, and you can go home in peace...or, in Rick's case, loneliness.

The evenings were bad enough for Rick, but the weekends were endless, and they soon drove him back onto the campus where, after a little break, he found a warm welcome from the old crowd. He was welcomed as a novelty rather than as a "has been," particularly since he had a steady source of income and was old enough now to legally purchase alcohol. The underclassmen valued this resource at their parties, and after several weeks spent alone with his sense of failure, Rick enjoyed being their hero, however mercenary their acceptance.

———

Toby also found himself driven by the quest for approval. His life was controlled by the desire to have his "sacrifice" validated. He constantly found new ways to demonstrate his commitment to the farm. He had taken over the entire dairy operation and milked every morning and every evening for 415 days without a break. He used his own money to send his parents on a vacation that winter, knowing that as the story got out, the friends and gossips would not fail to notice that it was the result of his "sacrifice." He stopped going out with his high school friends and rarely went to town unless he was on a mission for the farm. He knew that the farmers he would see at the elevator or the oil cooperative would recognize in him the commitment to the farm, which they all secretly wished their sons had shown. He was a living reminder that some sons were willing to sacrifice a life of excitement, even if their sons weren't.

Rose and Willard initially appreciated the ease that Toby's work granted them, but gradually they became concerned. Rose would search the papers for events in the community that Toby might like to attend, but milking makes a good excuse to avoid them. Even though Willard would happily have done the chores, Toby would never let him and risk losing tomorrow's count of 416 consecutive days.

Spring came, and Rick realized that his intention to save money for school was not working well. He knew the problem was the parties, but he consoled himself that school was almost over. During the summer, he would make up for his lack of thrift. Going home from an end-of-year party, Rick got a DUI. He lacked the funds to bail out, and none of his friends, whose admiration he cherished, were around to help out. He sat in jail for long enough to lose his job. He forfeited his car and the fines with which he was sentenced erased any hope of saving for school.

Getting another job proved to be more of a problem than he expected. The police record severely limited his marketability for any higher-paying positions. Once a job was secured, he realized he couldn't afford his apartment. He found a room he could rent at half the cost but quickly realized that saving up for college was unrealistic. Reality for him was survival.

The sense of loneliness and failure were joined by the overwhelming feeling of shame. Rick might get his fines paid and get off probation, but the chance of ever going home was closed. He felt he could never face the hurt his choices had caused them.

It didn't help his economic situation that every couple of weeks, when he could no longer stand the pain, he would allow himself a vacation…with the bottle. He knew now that it was the alcohol that held him. Always before he argued with himself that it was the companionship he wanted—he didn't need the booze, but he liked the parties. Even now, he justified himself that he wasn't really drinking alone; he was just waiting till his friends came back in the fall. But no matter what defensive gymnastics he attempted or how sufficiently he deadened his conscience, the economics of his habit were bringing him further and further down.

He rented his room for cash from an unscrupulous landlord whose buildings were probably condemned but allowed to stand by the city council lest the homeless blight the appearance of their fair city. Showers did not function, and people used the toilets whether they functioned or not. Rick did his best to maintain his level of hygiene and personal appearance, but the hardest thing was caring.

His binges were using up the options for entry-level jobs. Not many employers take a chance on high-risk employees. Through the summer, he hoped he might get help from some of his college friends when they returned in the fall. But after several unsuccessful attempts to crash the old party scene, he realized that more of his former popularity was based on the money he spent than he had ever been willing to admit.

His life continued spiraling downward. Finally, he ended up with a job at a fast-food restaurant. Regular fast-food positions are entry-level jobs; they teach young people to work and incentivize them to move on to bigger and better things.

Rick wasn't in a job like that. He was in a cheap imitation of the real fast food places. It was an establishment called Bozo Burgers which, in the 1970s, had tried to compete with McDonald's spokesclown, Ronald. It failed miserably. Its clown motif was lost on its clientele. They came to Bozo Burgers because it was cheap. The biggest boost to its revenues came as a result of its hours. It was located in an old part of town, so it didn't have to compete directly with its fast food rivals along the highway; its neighbors were mostly bars. By staying open until 4 am, they could feed the people forced onto the street by the closing of the bars.

The job had several advantages for Rick. He worked until closing most nights, which meant his sleep time was in the day. This helped Rick stay away from the people who would draw him to alcohol. He still slipped back occasionally, but he was never so drunk by 8 pm. that he couldn't go to work. And for the owner of Bozo Burgers, coming to work drunk wasn't serious enough to fire you; he didn't exactly have lines of people waiting to work there. Rick was holding his own.

Financially, he had worn out the patience of the probation officer, so most of Rick's check had to go directly to the county if he didn't want to go back to jail. Rick would have gone hungry many days, but since he closed the restaurant, he could take home any food left on the warming racks when it was time to clean up. He would ride his bike home around 5 am clutching the bag of cold Bozo Burgers that meant he would eat for another day, dead tired, lonely, and hopeless.

Then they found him. The freshman class that admired him so much when he would provide the booze for their parties had come of age. They were no longer limited to the parties on campus where the administration would turn a blind eye to their minority. Now, they were free to patronize the town bars. One night after closing down the place next door, a carload of college kids swung into the Bozo Burgers drive-thru and ordered something to take the edge off their post-partying hunger. When they pulled up to the window, it took them a minute to recognize who it was standing there in the polka-dotted visor with the clown nose on the brim.

Drunk people are poor judges of what is funny, although the Bozo Burgers head gear was admittedly a bit ridiculous, his drunk friends thought it was hilarious. Rick hoped that, in their condition, they might forget all about him by morning, but he had no such luck. The story spread, and that segment of the campus who remembered Rick made Bozo Burgers a regular stop when they wanted to extend their carousing beyond closing time.

Eventually, the novelty of Rick's absurd position wore off. Rather than go elsewhere, Rick's "friends" thought up a new game. The construction of the drive-thru made it easy to pull away from the restaurant unseen. A carload of obnoxious drunks would place a full order, circle around the back of the next-door building, pull across the street, and watch. If no one else came, they would get to watch Rick standing there with a bag full of Bozo Burgers, waiting. It was even funnier when another car pulled up after them. There would be an argument about the order, and as often as not, at least some of the occupants of that car were drunk too.

They thought this was hilarious. Rick was grateful when the college crowd left for the summer. He earnestly hoped that by fall, he would be forgotten. He wasn't.

———————

He hadn't been forgotten at home, either. Three and a half years had passed since they had heard from Rick. That was the last quarter that money had been paid to the college. Since then, there has been no contact. Willard and Rose carried their concern with them all the time. They only told their closest friends, but the story trickled out, confirmed by the apparent worry etched into Rose and Willard's faces. Toby basked in a new wave of homage to the perception of his sacrifice. He pushed himself relentlessly to present himself as the martyr designate of the Teply family.

The concern over Rick's waywardness escalated through a chain of events that summer. Rose's brother-in-law (who tended to be a worrier and cherished passing "concerns" on to those around him) had been watching the news one evening when there was a report on a major train collision/derailment in Maxwell, California. The deceased driver of the car was listed as unidentified, but the remains of the vehicle, clearly shown on the news report, could easily be identified as a blue Pontiac Grand Am. He called Rose to share his concern, and over the next few days, she tried to find a follow-up story on the Internet. She had no success, and her call to the Maxwell police was only forwarded to four different people before she got a half-hearted promise to "check into that for you."

Willard tended to dismiss the idea that Rick was the driver. After all, Maxwell was almost sixty miles from the college, and the Grand Am was hardly an unusual make. However, a seed was planted in their minds, which was difficult to completely uproot, especially the following week when they received a phone call from someone at the California Motor Vehicle Department. The agent wished to speak to Rick. When Rose said he wasn't available, she was asked if she knew whether the vehicle had been sold. When Rose tried to discover if the call was prompted by something serious, the agent could not or would not answer.

She could not know, nor could Rose, that the question was prompted by a speeding ticket that got misdirected due to a problem with the registration of Rick's Grand Am, which had been sold at a police auction.

The evidence was far from conclusive, but Willard and Rose had to face the fact that Rick might be dead, and they might never know with certainty. Their hearts were broken even though they cherished faint gleams of hope. Toby felt the sorrow, too, but it was outweighed by a new tenderness shown to him by his parents and those close to them.

The fall quarter had hardly begun when Rick began getting visits from the old friends. His life had stabilized at an incredibly low point: work and sleep and cold Bozo Burgers with a side of cold fries. He had just paid off his last fine and had been able to buy a better bike. Not only was it transportation, it was sanity as well. He biked every day and found that the exercise kept him away from the alcohol. He would ride for several hours in the afternoon, then stop at a rundown truck stop where he could shower for $1.50, then go to work.

One night, just before closing time, there came a suspect order. Someone at the drive-thru ordered eight Bozo Bonus Burger meals. Rick had gotten an instinct for these things. He thought it was his "friends," but what could he do? He was working alone, so he couldn't send someone out to check the drive-thru lane, and he had a customer waiting at the counter. He went ahead and dropped the extra fries and assembled the burgers. When no car appeared, he wasn't shocked. What surprised him was that shortly after he had shut off the outside lights, locked up, and begun cleaning the grill, the owner showed up. His inspections were rare, and his standards were low, but he was driven by greed. Rick didn't like him, but he had never had trouble with him before. The owner toured the restaurant and was satisfied until he saw the eight Bozo Bonus Burger meals. Immediately, he suspected that Rick was purposely over-cooking at closing time.

"What are these doing here?" he questioned Rick, who was still scraping on the grill.

"What?" Rick asked, looking up.

With a marked edge to his voice, he pointed at the smiling face of Bozo on the bag of burgers and said, "These."

Rick, wearing the grease-stained apron reserved for scrubbing the grill, holding the grill stone in his rubber-gloved hand, dripping with sweat and spattered from the cleaning process, stepped over to where the owner was standing. He caught sight of the bag with the burgers and fries and answered, "We had another drive-off."

"Just minutes before you quit? How convenient." The accusation was thinly veiled, and something in Rick reached a tipping point.

"Do you think I am stealing Bozo Burgers?"

The owner backpedaled a bit, "I didn't say that; I just meant, you have to admit it looks suspicious."

Rick reached down and began untying his apron. "I want to tell you something. I have done a lot of things I regret, but I have never stolen from anyone. And if I were going to steal something, the last thing in the world I would steal is a Bozo Burgers. You can take this apron, these gloves, this stone and this stupid hat. I quit." Rick turned and started walking.

"Wait, I didn't mean it! I need you to finish closing." Rick was taking his coat from the hook. "You can't just walk out. Look, finish up here, and when you come to the office tomorrow for your check I'll give you a raise," the owner offered pressing the bag of burgers into Rick's hands.

"Don't bother, you won't see me ever again." Rick zoned out the further offers and protests while he unlocked his bike, put the burgers in his backpack, and rode off.

—————

All night, Rick rode, unaware of where he was going, but certain that he would never return to that job, that town, or the disgusting room he had called home. There had to be a life worth living somewhere, and he, as he grew more fatigued, felt that as long as he kept riding, he might be getting closer to finding it. Despite his initial interest in going to California, he had never really seen much of the state, so by morning, he was in thoroughly unfamiliar territory. The land began rising out of the valley into the foothills. Before him, he could begin to make out details in the mountain that, for the last few years, had been an unnoticed smudge on the horizon. Reaching the crest of one of these foothills, he finally felt like he could stand to stop and take a rest. He left the bike in the ditch and climbed a little higher up the bank at the side of the road to where he could look back over the valley behind him. He leaned back on the hillside and rested, looking at the sky and the clouds and the valley stretching below him.

The emotional stress, the sleepless night, and the long bike ride disposed him to close his eyes and let his mind drift. He woke two hours later with the sensation that he was waking up from a dream. It had been several years since sleep had given him rest. He sat up and looked down into the valley that stretched out of sight.

The land was laid out in the familiar patchwork of cultivated fields. It was harvest time, and although he couldn't easily recognize the crops, he could recognize the combines making their rounds. To his left, he could see two combines working in the adjacent fields: one John Deere green and one Case/IH red. In his mind, he could hear the arguments that would pass for camaraderie between the two neighbors. Spirits would be high. They always were during the harvest, which meant more of the never-ending friendly chaffing.

The scene recalled him back to his home. Everyone was busy during the harvest and racing to get the grain into storage before some freak weather event could undo their summer of work and investment. But with every round, the trucks drove away with load after load of return on that investment. His father had always hired extra help to ensure nothing could interrupt the work. In the years before Rick took his place as one of the drivers, he spent the harvest jumping from one vehicle to the next. After riding for a while in the combine, he would catch a ride on one of the trucks going to the elevator. While waiting in line to unload,, the driver, an uncle or a hired hand, would inevitably spring for a can of pop from the old machine in the weight office. As a young man, he always looked forward to the week or two he spent in fellowship with men who knew they were doing something significant—harvesting.

Days started early and continued into the night, but the highlight came at dinner—not the evening meal called "dinner" by people who just have a "lunch" at noon, but a real dinner. For an hour in the middle of the day, all the combines, trucks, and tractors were parked, and all the hands made their way to Rose's kitchen. Tables had been set up extending into the living room and the arriving workers would parade through the mudroom, emerging with clean hands and some percentage of the dust and dirt that had gathered on their faces removed. They would file to the table and sit down, waiting patiently until Willard bowed his head and gave thanks for the food, including a prayer for safety in the work still to be done. Then Rose would begin carrying dishes to the table. Roast, pork chops, meatloaf, roast chicken, or some other meat raised right on the farm; potatoes, either mashed or new from the garden; vegetables (green beans were Rick's favorite); coleslaw, macaroni or Jell-O salad; and desserts of a dozen different varieties. Everyone ate until they were stuffed, then, while the older set finished their cups of coffee (slowly, to rest just a bit longer), the younger help would gather out under the maple tree in the yard and sit in the grass.

Sitting on the hillside, Rick could almost imagine himself at home. It was still at least a month before the harvest would begin there. He knew he had given up any right to think of it as his home, but his dad would be hiring someone to work for him. Maybe he could get the job. Just being one of the hired help for two weeks would be better than anything open to him here. He realized it was even better than anything he had ever hoped to find. It had taken the worst to realize that what he had left behind was better than the best.

The following week was a blur. He found someone who would buy his bike for enough money to purchase a bus ticket. But the trip was far from direct. Cold Bozo Burgers, water from a drinking fountain, and the dream of going home sustained him through crowded bus rides and long layovers. He finally disembarked at the convenience store, which served as a bus station in his hometown. He still had twelve miles to get to the farm. Rick hoped to catch a ride but was reluctant to meet anyone from his past. He looked far different from when he left. His hair was long and pulled back into a ponytail, and he hoped the week plus of stubble would obscure his face. He knew the town too well to think that people wouldn't stare, but he hoped they wouldn't connect a suspicious-looking stranger with his real identity. Most of the people who turned to stare didn't, but as Rick walked by the café on the main street, a casual acquaintance of his father, Arnie Miller, was enjoying a cup of coffee and a piece of pie in the booth closest to the window. He wasn't close enough to the family to know that Rick wasn't expected, but seeing the young man reminded him that he wanted to ask Willard some questions about a hay cutter/conditioner listed in the classifieds a month or so ago.

He borrowed a phone book from the waitress and dialed the Teply's number. Rose answered and informed Arnie that Willard was taking lunch out to the field for Toby. A little polite conversation followed, and Arnie said, "I saw your son in town today."

"You're lucky," Rose quipped. "We can hardly get Toby off the farm. He's becoming a bit of a hermit."

"No, not Toby. It looked like Rick. I guess he's letting his hair grow out."

All the life was gone from Rose's voice when she answered, "I don't know. We haven't heard from Rick for years."

"Well, maybe it was someone else. I'll call Willard back some evening," said Arnie, sensing that he had brought up a painful subject and wishing to end the conversation.

Rose tried to pass the conversation off as insignificant but couldn't completely get over it. When she saw Willard's truck pull into the yard, she went out and told him about the call. "It's probably nothing. Arnie didn't know Rick that well," Willard responded. But Rose knew her husband well enough to realize he was forcing himself not to raise his hopes. As often as she caught sight of him from the window, she could see that he was unwilling to leave sight of the driveway.

Once Rick was out of town, he caught a ride for the seven miles to the west. The driver, who was not from the area, offered to take Rick the remainder of the journey, but Rick described the remaining five miles as "just a little way up the road" and claimed that he would "rather walk." Actually, he was getting nervous. The whole way home, he had been rehearsing the speech he would give. "Father, I made a mess of things. I don't deserve anything from you, but I was wondering if you needed an extra hand to work during the harvest." It seemed unlikely to him that his father would even consider this. By now, his father had to know that Rick had wasted all the money and that his letters and calls had been nothing more than a serialized lie.

As Rick trudged homeward, he encountered many sights that held memories for him: the woods where he shot his first deer and the culvert that became a fort for Toby and himself. The sweetness of the memories cut him to the heart because he knew they represented a life and an innocence he could never regain.

Willard had been puttering about the farm yard, trying to find tasks allowing him to keep watch for an arrival he forced himself to deny he was expecting. They would probably get a phone call someday that Rick if he was alive, was nowhere near here. But still, he could not pull himself away for long.

The rolling door of the machine shop had jammed, and Willard decided it was time to repair it, an activity that would take the long step ladder. The first step, however, was not to get the ladder but to remember where he had used it last. This required some wandering about the farm, and when he returned to the front of the shop with the ladder (which had been leaning on the back of the hay shed), he looked down the road and saw a figure walking alone. He couldn't identify any features, so he moved closer to the road. At each step, he expected to recognize the form as one of the neighbors, but as the figure drew near, he still could not be sure. The man was walking with his head down as if he was exhausted, like he carried a large burden in the backpack he was wearing. Then the man looked up, and Willard knew, perhaps more by mannerism than by sight, that it was Rick. Willard set the wrenches and the rag he was carrying in the newspaper delivery box as he passed it, and started running towards his son. He threw his arms around him and hugged him with all the pent-up emotion of years of waiting. Tears were streaming down his cheeks, and still, he held Rick close as if he would never let him go.

Muffled in his father's arms, Rick couldn't speak, and despite having prepared to make his passionless business proposition, he could not stop the tears from flowing down his dusty cheeks. Finally, his father held him away from his body to get a look at the son he had missed, and Rick began his speech. "Dad, I'm sorry, I made a mess of things. I don't deserve anything from you, but I know that the harvest is coming soon, and I thought you might be able to use more help."

Willard looked at him through the tears and said, "Rick, you are my son. Your place is in my family. Nothing you have done could ever change that. Welcome home." Rose met them at the end of the driveway, and the three of them proceeded to the house.

Now, as Rick had suspected, he hadn't gone unnoticed in town. The grapevine just took a while to connect Arnie's supposition with the unkempt young man. Once the connection was made, the story began to travel. As the story began to ripple through concentric circles of gossip, Rick was headed home. The problem sounded like something from a math book. "If a rumor travels at a rate of x, and a pedestrian travels at a rate of…." The result was that Willard and Rose's neighbors started to hear the news within minutes of Rick's arrival home. Now, even gossips have some etiquette. You can't just drive up to the house and demand to know what's going on, and only the most brazen will call and say, "I was just gossiping with my friend, and I heard…." The acceptable way to confirm a rumor is to conjure up a different reason to initiate some contact.

The first to do this was the neighbor to the west, who happened to remember a pair of jumper cables he had borrowed last winter. The neighbor to the east "happened to be taking a walk" and noticed some wrenches lying in the newspaper box and thought Willard might forget where he had put them. The phone calls and the visits started pouring in. The cause was transparent, and even though in the past Willard had complained about the "infernal gossips," today he didn't mind. He wanted the whole world to know the news, "My son is home!" Anybody who stopped by was invited into the house. The coffee maker and the old perk pot were going strong, and Rose had pulled out of the freezer the pans of bars she had made in preparation for the coming harvest meals. Anyone who shared Rick's expectation of a conditional acceptance could clearly see that such an idea never entered Willard or Rose's mind. Their son was home. Their joy was abundant.

The party was in full swing when Toby pulled through the yard with the tractor and a train of three forage wagons. He was a little put out that his father hadn't returned to get the wagons so he could keep chopping until milking time, but he knew something had probably come up. He couldn't imagine what it was when he saw the cars. He parked the train of wagons by the silage pit and headed to the barn. On the way, he called to someone heading to their pickup to leave, "What's going on in there?"

"Don't you know? Rick got home."

It was just as well that they were far enough from him not to see his reaction. Toby continued on his way to the barn and decided he would begin milking a bit early; anything to avoid going up to the house.

Willard had seen Toby's return and was anxious to see him. He had to apologize for not returning to the field, but he knew Toby would understand. Willard went from group to group of friends, visiting and sharing his joy, until, eventually, he found his wife in the kitchen and asked, "Has Toby come up to the house?"

"I haven't seen him," Rose answered.

One of the men standing within earshot suggested, "Check the barn. I think I heard the vacuum pump."

A few steps away from the house, Willard could hear the droning hum from the milk parlor, which meant Toby was milking. Willard got to the barn and walked into the parlor. The cows had filed in and were waiting to be milked. Willard helped wash the udders ahead of Toby, who attached the milking machines. They gave each cow a second scoop of grain, and then there was nothing else to distract them.

"Rick is home," Willard said.

"I know."

"What's wrong?"

Toby wanted to say "nothing," but he couldn't. The answer came in a flood of emotion. "Every morning. Every night. I come out here, sick or not. Every day. I haven't taken a vacation. I haven't taken a night off. Then, all day, I work, nothing but work. And not once have we had a party like this. Nothing. Do you know how much I have sacrificed to be here? But he waltzes home after costing you thousands of dollars, and you throw a party. Oh yay! Rick's home. Did it ever occur to you that I would have liked to go off and party and have a good time?"

The cow in the third stall, number 876, kicked off her milkers, and Toby went to put them on again. He came back to his father, who said, "I don't think you would have."

"Would have what?" asked Toby, who had forgotten the particulars of his speech.

"I don't think you would have liked to 'go off and party and have a good time.' I have watched you, Toby. I think you're making yourself miserable with the thought that you have had to give up something good. And now, when Rick has finally realized that what he really wanted was here, he is only returning to what you have always had. We are together, and everything that I have is yours. You lived life; he has lived death. Now, after we thought he was dead, he has come back to find life. He needs you to show him how to live. It's what I have longed for, and now that it has happened, can you rejoice with me?"

The tears came slowly for Toby, but nothing could stop them once they began. The years of posturing and pretending, the masks he had worn, and the lurking bitterness all seemed so empty compared to a love big enough for him and Rick. His father's arms were around him now, holding him tight as if he would never let him go.

Their tears fell together on the barn floor until 876 kicked off her milkers again. The cows still had to be milked. Willard helped until he felt ready to face the full house, and then he left Toby to finish.

Later, when everyone had gone home, Rose looked through the kitchen window and saw Toby coming in from the barn. Rick, who was helping his mother clean up, saw him too. He wiped his hands and went to the door. She watched him walking to meet his brother, shyly at first, until Toby started running. The two hugged, and even in the dim glow of the security light, she could see the tears glint off both their cheeks. Willard came up behind her and put his arms around her. She could feel his hot tears falling on her shoulder. "They're both home now."

Take a look at your own position
in relation to the Father.
Are you outside the Father's arms
longing to come into the Father's presence,
or are you inside looking out,
feeling that you are missing all the pleasures of this world?
Either way,
the Father wants you home.

No Fish

I love fishing and do it often enough to consider myself a fisherman. One of the truly great pleasures for a fisherman is to have a Secret Spot. Don't get me wrong, returning from an outing with a nice mess of fish is always rewarding, but I am not above making a detour past a neighbor's so I can show off the catch and hear the inevitable question, "Where'd you get 'em?"

However, the pleasure of such a question significantly increases if you can answer, "I caught 'em at my Secret Spot."

"Where's that?"

"I can't tell you." (*Pause for effect, continue in a whisper*) "It's a secret."

So, as a committed fisherman, I am always on the lookout, not just for good lakes to fish, but for a Secret Spot.

My first two sons were never particularly interested in fishing, but my third son, Wesley, loved it. So, it should be easy to imagine a time when he lived at home and, finding ourselves in the car together, we might have been induced to make detours, here or there, scouting the back roads of Clearwater County, Minnesota, for a Secret Spot.

Let's imagine further a day when we are returning from Detroit Lakes and decide to cut north from Highway 113 through the heart of the White Earth State forest. We enjoy the ride as we look for a likely spot to go fishing.

There is no lack of lakes on this stretch of road. However, most of the lakes we are passing are either:

1.) Too accessible to be a good Secret Spot. I mean, if anyone can get to the lake, then anyone can... well... get to the lake. A secret spot requires something to keep the average fisherman from easily getting to the lake or even knowing it's there.

Or,

2.) The lakes are too small. The cold winters in this northern climate put significant stress on the lakes. Once the weather turns cold and a layer of ice forms, the lake is sealed off from absorbing oxygen directly from the air. When the snows begin, the blanket on the lake blocks sunlight from entering the water, stopping photosynthesis. Photosynthesis allows a plant to store energy, but fortunately for us all, it also converts carbon dioxide into oxygen. This means that the two main sources of oxygen for a lake are reduced, if not totally stopped, in the winter.

Dead and dying vegetation in a shallow lake intensifies the problem because it uses much of the available oxygen in the decomposition process.

For the fish to survive in a lake in Minnesota, it must be big enough to store sufficient oxygen for the whole winter. From the moment the ice forms, the fish are in a race against time. Will spring arrive and open the lake before the oxygen runs out? If the winter kill didn't affect so many small bodies of water, the Minnesota license plate might need another zero, making the land of ten thousand lakes the land of a hundred thousand.

So, as my son and I scan the bodies of water we can see from the road, we are looking for just the right size lake—a lake small enough that most fishermen would assume it has no fish but which, for some reason, has an unexpected population. And if this Secret Spot happened to be difficult to reach with an expensive boat on a trailer, it would be all the nicer for those of us who are content to fish from a humble rowboat.

As we travel the road that winds through woods, Wes calls my attention to a trail leading off the road. It is little more than a footpath, but it appears to have been used occasionally by foot traffic, not by four-wheelers.

Ever since four-wheelers have become popular, every passable trail gets visited by roving gangs of ATV users who are just out for a ride. But this trail appears too narrow to easily accommodate a four-wheeler. Yet, since it appears to have had foot traffic, it must lead somewhere. It follows a general downward slope, which might indicate that it leads to a body of water. I look over at Wes, who nods his head, so I pull our pickup as far off the road as I dare and park.

We begin following the dim trail and, within a hundred yards, discover why no ATVs have driven the path. Two large trees lay across the trail, making it difficult for someone on foot, but impossible for someone on a wheeled vehicle to proceed. The footpath continues past the fallen trees so, we follow it.

It is hard to judge distance in the woods, particularly if the trail is constantly turning like this one, but after about half a mile, we suddenly descend a small hill and come out on the shores of a beautiful little lake.

The lake seems like the perfect Secret Spot. Off to my left stretches a large shallow bay with emergent weeds—the ideal habitat for largemouth bass. Then, where the bank gets steeper and the water darker, I can picture big walleyes cruising in the depth. To my right is a small island from which a tall white pine has fallen into the lake, reaching forty or fifty feet out into the water, creating the perfect habitat for crappies. And stretching out from the island's far side, a bed of reeds reaches almost to the cattails lining the shore. I can imagine the northern pike, with their voracious appetites, cruising the weed line there, just waiting for a tempting lure.

My son has made a similar survey of the lake. I turn and ask him the vital question.

"See any leech traps?"

No matter how much we may dream of finding a Secret Spot, we don't delude ourselves into thinking the leech trappers wouldn't have been their first. Early every spring, in this part of the state, an army of motivated outdoorsmen hit every pothole, pond, and puddle within miles, hoping to trap leeches to sell to one of the bait buyers in the area.

Leeches can survive in lakes that don't even maintain sufficient oxygen for minnows, let alone for game fish. So, no body of water is too small to consider as a potential leeching spot. Many trappers use heavy plastic perforated bags baited with a piece of beef kidney or other offal and anchored with a rock as their trap, but tied to one corner by a piece of twine, they will have a small square of Styrofoam which helps them locate the trap and serves as a handle to pull it up from the depths.

Most lakes have some leeches, but in lakes with a healthy population of hungry fish, leeches will be fairly scarce. Such lakes are not worth trapping. A fishless lake, on the other hand, can turn into a real gold mine for a trapper.

We scan the lake again, focusing on the edges, but find none of the telltale Styrofoam pieces bobbing on the water. That's a pretty good sign that the lake has at least enough fish to keep the leech population down.

Wes's eyes shine as I turn to him and inquire, "What do you think? Shall we come back and see what we can catch here?"

"Yeah. Can we come right back?"

I suggest, "I think we should get things ready tonight and come back early tomorrow morning."

With a farewell glance, we turn around to find the trail back. Suddenly, Wes points to a tree.

"Look!"

He is pointing at a sign nailed to the trunk of a red oak tree growing by the path. Actually, only half of the sign remains. A branch which has fallen from the tree has knocked the other half to the ground. What's left reads "NO FIS…"

Wes looks at it with discouragement, "What do you think it said?"

"It must have said 'NO FISHING' before it got hit," I respond.

"Doesn't that mean we can't fish here?" he asks, puzzled by my wide smile.

"No, son, I think this means it's someone else's Secret Spot. They just put that sign there to try to keep us from finding out how good it is."

"But it says we can't fish here," he protests.

"Don't worry about that," I assure him, "I know for a fact that we have as much right to be here as anyone else. This is public land, so no one can just nail up a sign and keep us from fishing here."

"Are you sure?"

"We'll check the map tonight, but I'm sure this is all public land, so whoever put that sign there is just trying to scare us away."

Early the next morning, we pull up to the head of the trail with our rowboat loaded onto the back of the pick-up. After a long discussion, we decided that even though it would be easier to drag the canoe into the lake, the rowboat is a better craft for catching lots of big fish.

Wesley is carrying the fishing rods, the oars, and one tackle box. With my life jacket buckled over his, he looks like a kid bundled into a snowsuit, his arms sticking almost straight out at his sides.

I am dragging the boat. The sun is just rising so the day hasn't really warmed up yet, but by the time I reach the log obstacle, I am already drenched in sweat. We get the boat over the two logs about the same time that the deer flies wake up. For the rest of the journey, I have to stop every few minutes to add a layer of Deep Woods OFF bug repellent, which the flies treat as a sort of garnish—although they might not want to eat it, it makes the main entree that much more appealing.

Only the thought of the fish we will be catching, and the smug satisfaction we will get not telling anyone about our Secret Spot, keeps us going.

Finally, we descend the last hill, and I drag the boat to the edge of the lake. We place everything in the boat, then I take a minute to select a lure. I want to be ready to start catching fish the minute we hit the water. Wes already has his rod set up. I lean down to dig in my tackle box for just the right bait.

"What are you using?" I question my son.

"Do you even have to ask?" Wesley always starts with a lip-less crankbait.

"So, you think the old rattle trap is the thing today?" I comment, selecting a quarter-ounce black spinner bait with shiny Colorado blades.

Instead of an answer, he clears his throat, and I look up to see that we are not alone.

My first impression is that an old man has stepped out of the woods next to us. But I realize he may just appear old because of the floppy felt hat and the large beard covering his face. Immediately, I suspect that we are about to meet the man who put up the sign. However, I carefully checked the county plat book the previous evening, so I know we are allowed to fish here. I confidently greet him as if nothing, whatever, is the matter.

"Good morning! Beautiful day, isn't it?" I suggest with exaggerated cheerfulness.

"It sure is," he replies, matching my cheerful tone. "Flies are bad though. They hang out in the shade waiting to ambush you."

"And I think the smell of Deep Woods OFF just stimulates their appetite."

The woodsman chuckles and finally gets to the point. "What are you fellows planning to do?"

"We're going see if we can't catch some fish," I reply, still trying to maintain a confident tone.

"That's what it looks like." He comments, "Didn't you see the sign?"

His tone is more curious than accusatory, so I try to keep any defensiveness out of my voice. "Yep, we did. Apparently, someone thought they could keep us from fishing public waters by just tacking up a homemade sign," I explain, making sure he knows that his bluff won't work on us. For good measure, I add, "I checked it out on my county map last night to be absolutely certain."

He looks increasingly puzzled, "Are you sure you saw the sign?"

By now, my efforts at remaining calm are failing, so I answer a little more sharply, "Look, I saw the sign, but no one, including you, can keep us from fishing public waters."

"I'm not trying to keep you from fishing. I just thought that if you had seen the sign…"

I didn't wait for him to finish. My defenses were up, I hated for my son to see me speak so bluntly to a stranger, but he would understand that I was just boldly standing up for what was right.

"I don't know what you are trying to pull, but I am fully within my rights as a citizen to fish here or on any other lake that belongs to the State of Minnesota. No one can stop me or harass me. I am licensed, my boat is properly registered, and we have the required life jackets, so there is no way you are going to stop us from fishing this lake with that sign!" I finish, pointing at the broken sign for dramatic effect.

Instead of answering, the gentleman walks over to the tree where the sign is nailed. He examines the sign and then begins kicking over the weeds and branches at the trunk of the tree. After a moment's search, he finds what he is seeking. He bends down and retrieves the second half of the sign from the ground.

Reaching up, he pushes that half against the half nailed to the tree. The fibers of wood where the sign had broken hold the sign in place for a moment, and my son and I can read it.

It simply says, "NO FISH."

The man watches the message slowly register on our faces and then speaks. "I walk by here a couple times a week. This spring, when the ice went out, I saw that all the fish had died. I put up the sign hoping it would save people the work of dragging a boat all the way in here just to find out there are No Fish.

"No Fish" and "No Fishing" sound quite similar.
Is it possible that, even though God has
Every right to demand our obedience,
Because He sees what is below the surface,
He actually gave us his law out of love,
To warn us.

God hates our sin,
Not because he is vindictive or insecure,
But because he knows the pain his children will face
As we discover that no matter what we think,
Or how hard we try,
We cannot make our way work,
When there are no fish.

Seeds

Pastor Charles Gleason didn't really like his title. He had to admit that, since he was hired by a church to give messages on Sunday mornings, he was, in fact, a "pastor," but he always invited people to call him Charlie. He hadn't particularly liked that name as a pre-teen because he thought it made him sound like a little boy. Now, he hoped it made him sound like a friend and less like a Pastor, or worse Reverend. To honor the wishes of some parents who were teaching their children to incorporate respect for their elders as part of their habit of behavior, Charlie offered "Mr. Charlie" to the children of his church as a title both respectful and familiar.

Some people in the congregation refused to drop the title, Pastor, even slightly resenting the affront to the dignity that they were convinced that the church should maintain, but whenever Charlie caught them using his unwanted title, he would watch doubly close for a chance to serve them in some profound way. Charlie believed that standing knee-deep in a flooded basement or lying under a car covered in grease makes it easier to drop the pretentious title. The strategy worked well when it was tried, but there were still some in the congregation whose lives were so well-ordered that Pastor Charles had not found the chance to convince them he was Charlie.

Although the church was somewhat divided on this point, everyone in town knew him as Charlie. And everyone, or almost everyone, in the town of about 1500 residents, knew him by sight. A significant majority considered him a friend. He made no distinction whatsoever between his congregants and those who had never entered his (or any other) church. To him, they were in the category of neighbors, which was Biblically far more significant than any human concept of parishioners or congregants. He made a point of befriending them in such a way that there was no spoken, or implied, obligation to attend his church. His friendship with the other clergy in the town testified to their trust that he wasn't out to steal from their flock. At the personal request of families, he had participated in funerals in every one of the churches in town.

As a matter of fact, one of his closest friends was Father Matthew, the priest at Saint Thaddeus' Catholic church. You didn't notice the close friendship in the warm greeting they exchanged—Charlie met everyone with the same enthusiasm. Their genuine friendship was evident in the way they teased each other. Giving each other a hard time was part of every conversation. They were both avid fishermen. Any time Charlie started to report on his fishing successes, Father Matthew would jokingly offer to bring back the church policy of selling indulgences so that Charlie could lie about the size of his fish with a clear conscience.

One source of constant chaffing for Father Matthew was the Catholic traditional acceptance of para-mutual gambling, or in plain terms, Bingo. The two men would good-naturedly go back and forth about the issue of gambling. Their friendly discussions would usually end in the same place: Charlie would suggest that if Father Matthew really thought God would supply for his church through gambling, he ought to spend the church money on a Powerball ticket, trusting God to reveal to him, or his pope, a winning number.

Father Matthew would reply, "And if a winning ticket turned up in your offering plate, are you saying your church wouldn't take the money?"

Which is why, when a Powerball lottery ticket appeared in the offering plate on the first of April, Charlie knew exactly whose April Fool's joke it was. The trustee who counted the offering handed the ticket to him, and Charlie tacked it to the bulletin board in his office with a big smile. Loving your neighbor was the most rewarding thing a person could do.

He promptly forgot the ticket, not even knowing precisely what a person did when they had a ticket. To him, it was just the memento of his friendship with Father Matthew. The night for the Powerball drawing came without fanfare since the eleven million dollar pot wasn't particularly noteworthy. Even Father Matthew had no idea that the ticket was a winner since he hadn't bothered to remember the numbers on the ticket, which he had folded between a dollar bill and sent to Charlie's offering with a mutual friend. It took a week for the news of the unclaimed lottery ticket, which had been sold in their area, to come to Father Matthew's attention. He began to suspect that he might know where the winning ticket was. However, he couldn't directly ask Charlie without admitting that he had donated the ticket.

Finally, curiosity got the better of him, and he paid a visit to his friend, under the guise of discussing the upcoming fishing season opener. Sitting in his friend's office, he caught sight of the Powerball ticket tacked to the bulletin board. He pointed to the slip and, feigning innocence, asked, "Hey, what's that? I thought you didn't go in for the lottery."

"Like you don't know where that came from," replied Charlie accusingly.

"Who me?" smiled Father Matthew. "So, was it a winner?"

"Don't know, don't care," asserted Charlie.

"Really? You aren't even a little curious?"

"I haven't even thought about it. Nobody ever wins those things. I mean, someone does, but what are the chances?"

Father Matthew was impressed that his friend didn't seem to care, but his curiosity was growing about the ticket. "Would you be a little more curious if you knew that the winning ticket was sold at the same store where that ticket was purchased, and that, so far, no one has come forward to claim the prize?"

"It would only make me curious to know how you would know where the ticket was purchased," claimed Charlie. But, by that evening, he had to admit that wasn't actually true. What if he had a winning ticket? What would he do? Or, more appropriately, what would the church do? What would he advise them to do?

Charlie had so far avoided any involvement with the Internet. On the occasions when some information was only available on the web, he would call his daughter and ask her to look it up, which she was happy to do. However, when he asked her to print off the information and send it to him in the mail, she would inevitably offer to help him get set up with e-mail access.

That night, it wasn't necessary. She looked up the winning numbers and confirmed over the phone that the church had received an eleven-million-dollar ticket in the offering plate. It would have made a great story for a media outlet. "Priest donates millions in protestant collection Plate." "Winning ticket, no April Fools Joke." But Charlie made his daughter promise not to tell anyone about the ticket until he had a chance to announce it to the church.

Charlie kept the secret for another week until there was a regularly scheduled deacon's meeting at the church. He spent that week praying and discussing with his wife Ann every imaginable use for the money. He didn't want to decide for the church, but he also knew that the board members trusted him, so he wanted to have his best suggestion prepared when he told them of the new challenge facing the church. By the time of the Tuesday evening board meeting, he had a suggestion.

After they had covered the standard decisions required for running the church, Charlie introduced the new topic. The first round of questions was primarily devoted to disbelief. Charlie was able to convince them that the ticket was real and the jackpot was theirs.

The next questions were devoted to how the ticket had ended up in the offering plate, which Charlie would not divulge. He had called Father Matthew to specifically ask him if he would accept all or part of the eleven million dollars if the church voted to give it back to him.

Father Matthew had chosen anonymity rather than accepting the windfall, "Besides," he added, "If the Good lord wants to test you with mammon, who am I to let you off the hook."

Charlie informed the board that since the ticket had been given anonymously, it would not be appropriate or possible to find out who contributed or to return the ticket. There seemed to be no question that they would have to take responsibility for the money, but there was a distinct question of whether they should accept the money as God's provision for the church. Was this a blessing or a test?

Charlie was proud of the men on the board, as one by one, they decided that they didn't want the money to go to the operation of the church. Gordon, a farmer and one of the deacons who normally talked very little, summed it up this way: "I know we could do a lot of nice things around here with the money, but I'm pretty sure everyone would see this as the church the lottery built, not the church Jesus built. We could argue that Jesus blessed us with the winning ticket 'til we were blue in the face, but I'm thinking no one, including me, would be convinced."

Once that question was settled, discussion moved on to what to do about the ticket. Even if the lottery didn't seem like God's way of providing for his church, it didn't mean that they should not collect. God might want them to make use of the money another way.

Again, Gordon's voice of reason focused the issue: "There's not much use discussing whether or not we <u>should</u> do something until we figure out what we <u>could</u> do. Any ideas?"

Charlie had let the conversation progress with little input, but now he stepped in, "I realize that I have had more time to think about this than the rest of you, but I have an idea."

The men were eager to hear, so Charlie began, "I started looking at non-profit corporations and asked myself a couple of questions, 'Could we do what they are doing?' And 'Would we be making people more dependent on our organization?' The type of organizations that stood out to me were those making micro-loans?"

Charlie went on to describe the work of several foundations that would make money available to aspiring entrepreneurs in third-world countries. The loans were small, but if they were used wisely, they could be a chance to get out of subsistence living. It might purchase a sewing machine, allowing a housewife to make a niche product or a computer to connect to the internet so an entrepreneur could offer their product to the whole world. The key was that the loan had to be limited to make it more valuable as a start on a new venture than as a subsidy of their current mode of living."

"Would we give our money to a microloan company, or would we send someone to a third-world country to distribute the funds?" asked one of the Deacons, obviously interested in the concept.

"Neither. We would do the same thing here."

"Make microloans in our community? Why? People can get help in many places," countered another on the board. "It almost seems like people can get too much help; they look to human services instead of looking at what they could do to fix their problems."

"True," agreed Charlie. "Often, the way to qualify for much of the help available is to have made a mess of your life. The deeper you have dug your hole, the more help you qualify for. Our system makes it easier to take the ten steps down to qualify for help than to make the two steps up to succeed.

"But what I am wondering," continued Charlie, "is, what if we could find a way to offer them help climbing instead of incentivizing their slide."

"Kind of a 'teach a man to fish' idea," suggested Gordon.

"Exactly," affirmed Charlie, "but if I had said that, no one would have believed I was speaking metaphorically."

Much discussion followed, but it mostly concerned ironing out the details. The decision was essentially made to attempt to invest the money in neighbors.

They decided to make the loans all of one size. Any person could write a business proposal and submit it to the church. If the board judged that the plan could be attempted with a five thousand dollar budget, the person would receive a check, and the money would be theirs to use for the next ten years. After ten years, the money would be repaid, but the church didn't want to be paid back; the money would be paid forward. The recipient would be responsible for finding another prospective entrepreneur in whom to invest. The men realized this provision would be hard to enforce, but they weren't all that sure they would even try. Besides, it wouldn't come into effect for ten years, so they could cross that bridge when they came to it.

There was one other provision of the loan. They asked the recipients to write a monthly update. It was nothing formal, just a letter describing what they had done with their business during the previous month. Each month the church received a letter, they would knock fifty dollars off the loan, so a conscientious debtor would end the ten years owing nothing, as long as they had stayed regularly in touch with their lender. Those letters were the heart of the program.

Nothing had an overtly spiritual dimension, a fact that bothered several of the church leaders, but Charlie explained it this way. "Everyone talks about believing in God as if that is the big challenge, but the amazing thing is that he believes in us. If we find a way to tangibly demonstrate that we believe in people, we can trust God to help them see it is just a faint picture of his confidence in them."

The board asked Charlie to take on the responsibility of organizing their lending venture, and surprisingly, Gordon volunteered to assist. Charlie knew it would be mostly paperwork and didn't think the farmer would enjoy that. He was right, but at least Gordon was usually there to keep Charlie company when they worked on the loans.

———

Things started slow because they chose not to advertise their loans. They trusted mostly word-of-mouth referrals, although the local paper wrote a story about how the church was using the money, which led the local radio station to follow up on the story with an interview. Business plans began trickling in and then increased to a steady flow. It took a year for the money to run out.

By that time, the letters were flowing back, bringing all manner of reports. A small amount of the jackpot had been used to equip a room in the church as a makeshift office. Charlie, who still managed to run everything without a computer, had furnished the room with a desk, several chairs, and a wall of filing cabinets. He would spend two days a week reviewing the mail they received and filing the reports in the proper folder. As often as he could, Gordon would join him, and the two men would read the stories of their investment in people. They would read every letter and send a postcard with a few words of encouragement so that those who continued to write would know that their letters were being read.

Many didn't write. They simply got too busy to even stay in touch with their benefactors. It didn't bother Charlie much; he had enough to read with those who did write, but he couldn't help being sad. He doubted that the monthly letters ending was because they had figured out that collection on the debt was legally uncertain. He thought it much more likely that the individuals were struggling to keep believing in their potential. Even if there was nothing but failure and disappointment to report, if you could talk about it, it was clear that you still believed it was temporary; when you hid from it, you were basically admitting it was there to stay.

When he could find time, he would go through the files and write notes of encouragement to those who had stopped writing, but he never knew whether it served to encourage them or was taken as an implied condemnation of their failure.

In the seasons when farm work kept Gordon busy, Father Matthew would often visit Charlie and help him review letters. The priest was sincerely impressed that the jackpot hadn't changed his friend, and even though he didn't challenge a long-standing tradition like Bingo, he was forced to think carefully about the role of personal faith in the parish's finances.

Then, one day in February, when Charlie was out fishing on the ice, the fish house he was helping a friend move slipped and crushed Charlie's ankle. The pain subsided quickly, but the doctor warned him that the ankle needed two weeks of complete rest. He knew Charlie well and guessed that the first day he allowed his patient to do what he could bear, Charlie would be back to a full schedule, so he forbid him to be up, even with crutches, more than twenty minutes daily.

In a breach of HIPAA requirements, the doctor enlisted the aid of his priest, Father Matthew, to try to convince Charlie to really, truly rest. Knowing his friend as he did, he doubted his advice would get further than the doctor's had, so the priest played a different gambit.

⸺⸺⸺

Charlie was down in the loan office on Monday morning, resting his foot while he caught up on the mail. Father Matthew stopped by, took one look at the pile of letters, and realized that in about two hours, Charlie would be finished and in great danger of talking himself into going for a walk.

"So what has all this taught you?" he asked, indicating the row of file cabinets.

Charlie looked up and answered, "Don't try to start a restaurant with only five thousand dollars." he held up the current letter as if it was evidence of the conclusion.

"No, I mean overall, what are the lessons to be learned?"

Charlie hadn't really thought about it. He had taken each letter independently without looking for trends or lessons and admitted as much to his friend.

"If a noble and generous friend had given me a chance to learn an eleven million dollar lesson, I hope I would at least make an effort to draw a worthwhile conclusion," opined the priest

"You gave me a two-dollar ticket as an April fool's joke, and now I spend half my life down here in the basement writing postcards," countered Charlie.

"You have my deepest sympathy," Father Matthew said to his friend, but the germ of an idea had been skillfully introduced. The next time he stopped to check on his friend, he found the desks piled high with folders waiting to be reviewed.

Re-reading each file chronologically gave a different perspective compared to reading all of the letters as they came. Charlie became engaged in piecing together the narrative of each loan they had made.

As he read, he discovered some distinct categories in the stories the correspondence told.

He began reading the files, starting with the earliest ones to go dormant. The first category that became evident he called the Frittered. These people had received their money and, for some reason, put off actually beginning their business. But, while they waited for whatever it was that would get them started, the money would fritter away. It wasn't caused by bad decisions or foolish spending; just a little got spent here and a little there, resulting in insufficient funds to begin the project. The money had been frittered away. Unfortunately, while the individual waited to accumulate enough to make a new start, the frittering process seldom could be stopped.

In a way, he felt sorry for these prospective entrepreneurs because it seemed like no matter what you did, there were always forces hovering around the edges, demanding or sneaking away with a little bit here and there. Charlie thought that if something had demanded the whole amount, these people could have resisted the temptation. The evidence seemed to bear that out. As far as he knew, no one had taken the money and bought something like a nice fishing boat, which would have been the temptation he would have faced. They resisted the frontal attack but lost the battle against the host of little things that nibbled at the seed money from which they planned to grow a small business.

If they had attempted something…, anything…, they might have made it, but they left the money lying where it frittered away.

Charlie dubbed the second category to give up the Facade. To begin with, these were the most exciting letters to read. Some people really longed to own their own business. Unfortunately, they seemed to value being recognized as businessmen and women more than they valued actually running a business. These were the people who, initially, sent copies of their new business cards with fancy full-color brochures. They purchased everything a new business owner would need to look like a business owner, the right clothes, the right technology, the right phone, rented the right office, and hired the right advertisers and web designers, but forgot to save any money to start doing business. Their facade sprang up, looking promising, but by the time the small investment money was gone, nothing productive was left. The businesses collapsed as quick as they grew, or quicker. The facades they had made for themselves became hideous caricatures of what a business person should be.

The third group was the most heartbreaking. The letters still trickled in, but they were tinged with a weariness for which Charlie felt a genuine sympathy. These businesses had been successful. The small start-up capital had been used to create a viable business venture, which grew and expanded until it came directly into competition with the realities of their life.

The successful proprietor was suddenly faced with a choice. What they had often started as a way to make a part-time income began to take on full-time obligations. The start-up had only required a low level of risk, a moderate level of effort, and if it didn't work out they could always return to their old job. Now, they had to choose. They either had to devote their whole life to the new business and quit their regular job or give up on the new and retreat to the comfort of the old life.

Or, they could try to do both. The ones that tried that were the most miserable; they were worn out. They tried to keep two things going, which both demanded total allegiance, and it was choking the life out of them. They were unwilling to give up the additional income because they could still remember what life had been like without it, but they were equally unwilling to sacrifice the sense of security their former career gave them. So they kept on trying to do both. And trying. And trying. They achieved everything Charlie would have hoped for and got none of the satisfaction of achieving it.

Then there was the last group. It was admittedly small, but the letters continued coming. Some of the people Charlie and Gordon had met personally. This group told a story of finding more than financial success; they had found a purpose.

One young man had bought a used trailer and a riding mower with the initial money. Two years later, he replaced the mower with a far nicer machine and gave the old mower to a young man who began his business with it. This new businessman had successfully built his company, paying the debt forward to another. Charlie had evidence of ten new businesses in direct lineage from the initial investment, and he suspected there were more that hadn't been mentioned in letters.

Another lady invested her money in a used sewing machine and all the thrift store prom dresses she could afford. Each spring, she didn't just sell refurbished prom dresses, she built relationships with hundreds of girls, for many, at the moment in their development when the decisions they made would guide the rest of their lives.

Garages and greenhouses, caterers and calligraphers, and any other kind of business you could or could not imagine were represented in the monthly reports in the final pile on Charlie's desk.

His foot was almost completely healed, and he had spent more time sitting in the past month than any time since he graduated from high school, but he was intrigued by the four piles. Looking at them he felt like it reminded him of something.... A story he knew well.... He had it now! He pulled a Bible out of a desk drawer and started paging through it, looking for the parable he was thinking of.

He was interrupted in his search by the arrival of Gordon, who had been coming in a bit more often to keep up with the current letters, while Charlie reviewed all of the files.

His old friend saw the four piles on his desk, and none left in the inbox, and asked, "So you finished them all, I guess? Learn anything?"

Charlie smiled and said, "I think so." He stuck his thumb in the Bible to save the page and explained the four piles: The Frittered, the Facade, the Weary, and the Fruitful, and apologized that they couldn't think of a good "F" for the third group.

"But it made me think of something," he said, "Listen to this:

> *...a sower went forth to sow; and when he sowed, some seeds fell by the wayside, and the fowls came and devoured them up; Some fell in stony places, where they had not much earth: and forthwith they sprung up because they had no deepness of earth: And when the sun was up, they were scorched; and because they had no root they withered away. And some fell among thorns; and the thorns sprung up and choked them; But other fell into good ground, and brought forth fruit..."*

Charlie sat thinking about the correlation, silently waiting for his friend's reply. When a minute passed and Gordon hadn't volunteered anything, Charlie looked over and saw a tear glistening on the old man's cheek.

Charlie thought the parallel between his piles and the two-thousand-year-old parable was striking, but he had not expected this reaction. He waited and watched his friend. Gordon looked up and saw Charlie watching him with a questioning gaze.

He reached up and brushed the tear from one cheek and then the other and finally, in answer to Charlie's look, said, "I don't run my farm this way."

Charlie's questioning look turned puzzled, and Gordon explained, "You may not know how much seeds cost, but when I plant, I make sure every seed goes into the good ground. I make sure I don't waste any in the weed line, on the rock pile, or on the road. The seeds only go into the good ground."

Charlie began to see the significance. How many times had he, or the church he served, decided who was 'good soil' and who wasn't? Had they made a distinction that the sower was unwilling to make?

He looked back up at Gordon. Tears were flowing again, but his friend continued, "I wouldn't be here today if Jesus hadn't thought it was worth wasting a few seeds on a stony weed-choked patch like me."

Inspectors

S ome people use the third person plural "they" or "them" in conjunction with shadowy conspiracies or nefarious hidden plots, but Duane Ponsford most often talked about "them" when he needed to get something fixed, as in "'They' said I needed a new transmission," or "'They' said it will cost $200 to fix the refrigerator."

Then, one day, he had an epiphany. He had just told his wife Sherry that he had taken their '74 Ford LTD to the shop, and "'They' said the car probably isn't worth fixing." She responded, "Who are 'They,' and how do 'They' know so much?"

That started Duane thinking; the life-changing idea he came up with didn't sound that profound. He simply realized, "'They' must have learned somehow, and 'They' probably aren't that much smarter than I am." Armed with this new conviction, he began to dare to do things a Junior High History teacher wouldn't normally be expected to do. Initially, the car and several home appliances received his inexpert attention. He met with mixed success, but on the whole, he managed to make things better more often than he made them worse. This emboldened him to take on more projects with the result that, a month after the birth of their daughter Melissa, he announced to Sherry, "I think I want to build us a house."

The two had been discussing purchasing a home and weighing the cost of ownership against the benefits of not throwing away a rent check every month, but Sherry wasn't expecting this. She didn't want to discourage Duane, but she knew it was a big jump from fixing her toaster to building a house. "Honey, are you sure you can manage a whole house?"

"No, but 'They' must have learned, and 'They' probably aren't that much smarter than I am.'"

Sherry leaned up and kissed him. "' They' probably aren't," she agreed, "I think you should go for it."

Two years later, Duane, Sherry, Missy, and a newborn son, Randy, moved into the house that Duane built. It wasn't finished, but it was very livable, and a year after the birth of their fifth child, Coleen, it was completely paid for. Coleen's first birthday cake had as its single candle a tightly rolled paper; the mortgage on their home. The house still wasn't finished, but it was livable, and over the next two decades, it was in a constant state of flux. Parts would get finished, parts would need to be repaired, changes in the family dynamics would call for the renovation of parts, and Duane executed all of these repairs and renovations by himself, with the help of his family.

He had learned a lot over the years and had become a very capable carpenter, just not a very conventional carpenter. The building trades have many conventions, not specifically about structural integrity or safety, but conventions that create a standard, allowing almost any carpenter to look at a job and know how the original structure was built. Duane didn't know a lot of those conventions, so the house he built was structurally safe but a bit unusual. Additionally, Duane's willingness to renovate whenever it appeared that the family could use the living space more effectively meant that the house wandered quite a ways from the industry standard. But Duane was proud of the house. It worked. There might be oddities and even some problems, but it had been a home for five wonderful children, and it was full of memories.

Small doors had been installed between the studs that had given the kids access to their rooms when they had converted part of the hallway into a rope walk when one of the girls started a macramé business. A second story had been added to the boy's room while they were still shorter than four feet. The attic allowed them to leave their legos out at night without the danger of a parent stepping on them in the dark. It was hard to stand in any room and not discover some structural innovation with an interesting story behind it.

But now, the nest was empty. Duane and Sherry had always assumed they would keep the house for the family to return to, but Missy had married a Farmer who lived about 20 minutes away. When the kids brought their families home, the farmhouse seemed better able to absorb the impact of five kids, five kids-in-law, and 21 grandkids than their home. Finally, Duane was forced to admit to himself that the house was more than they needed. He started to talk about needing to downsize. After years of watching Duane spend most of his free time working on housing projects, Sherry wanted him to have a break. The kids would have loved to help with the maintenance, but for all of them, their own children used up almost every minute of every day. So, even though no one was excited about saying goodbye to the house, everyone verbally supported Duane's decision.

He made a list of everything he wanted to do before he put the house on the market. He took one look, then tore up the list. He decided to sell the home "as-is." After all, why waste time doing a lot of projects that the buyer would immediately change? The house was solid and well maintained; he would stand by that; after all, it had been good enough for his whole family. There was no higher praise for a house in his mind.

The first week the house was on the market, the Realtor showed it to a young family. Duane and Sherry sincerely hoped the young couple would buy the house because they reminded Duane and Sherry so much of themselves. The husband even taught Social Studies, which was what they call history nowadays. The young family brought their newborn daughter along for a second viewing, and Sherry got to hold the baby while Duane took them on a more personalized tour of the house. The couple seemed very interested and talked like they intended to purchase the home, but that was before they spoke with their lender.

A first-time home buyer is likely to be very surprised at the amount of paperwork and the number of people whose permission is required to purchase a house. A day after their visit with Duane and Sherry, the young couple called to ask if they could have a building inspector come and inspect the home. They had been assured by the banker, who was planning to lend them the money, that it was just a formality. Still, it was required so that in the event the bank had to repossess the property, they wouldn't be stuck with a sub-standard building.

Duane agreed, and within a couple of days, he met the building inspector at his front door. He began his walk-through of the house; Duane soon discovered the man was a "hummer." He was professional, and that required that he not comment to the homeowner on his findings. He was supposed to dispassionately examine the structure and report on his findings. But he couldn't stop a low "Hmmm…" from escaping his vocal cords whenever he ran into one of Duane's functionally inspired renovations or utilitarian construction techniques.

In fairness to Mr. Hummer, he would have told anyone who asked that the building was functional and safe, but his job was to inform the banker how well it conformed to the industry standard--which it didn't. Duane watched as the inspector hummed his way through every single corner of every single room, stopping often to write on his clipboard.

The prospective buyers called Duane and Sherry a week later and asked if they could meet face-to-face. The two couples gathered at the kitchen table, and after a few minutes of small talk, the young husband slid a piece of paper across the table: "This is what I must agree to fix within the first year before the bank will lend me the money."

Duane began to feel some anger. The things on the list were fully functional. There was no good reason to rip out something that worked fine and replace it just to satisfy someone who would never set foot in the building. He looked up at the young couple.

"It seems like a pretty demanding list from someone who will never set foot in the building," commented the wife. "We would buy it today, but they won't lend us the money unless we promise to make these changes."

The husband took a breath and continued, "I have looked at our budget and crunched the numbers, and I am going to make an offer that I am ashamed to make. Before I do, I want you to know that I am not trying to lowball you, I will give you everything that I can afford, but I don't think I can afford to buy this place."

After hours of discussion, once the young couple had left, Duane and Sherry had to agree that the young man was right. As much as they would have liked to, they couldn't accept his offer. They called and broke the news to the couple and parted as friends. Both sides were sorry that the young couple simply didn't have the resources to purchase the house.

Two weeks went by before the next showing. This prospective buyer hoped to include the house in a series of rental properties he owned. He was pleasant to talk to and seemed very businesslike, but Sherry thought he was a little too slick. When pressed to justify her impressions, she withdrew them, but Duane had been married too long to ignore his wife's impressions. He would make sure he was cautious.

When the request came for a building inspection, Duane mentioned that one had been recently completed. That didn't satisfy the prospective buyer. It seemed he had his own inspector, whose opinion he trusted. Duane braced himself and agreed.

———

This second inspector was a "well" man. No hums, but when he caught sight of something unusual, he would limit his comment to a low "Well." He was even more thorough than the hummer. He examined every room and closet, tapping and feeling the walls. He climbed into the attic and crawled under the floorboards in the portion of the basement that only had a foundation. And every time he caught sight of unique carpentry, he would offer his comment, "Well."

Whenever he heard it, Duane wanted to justify himself and explain why he had built the way he had. He wanted to demonstrate that the area in question fully met any demand for strength put upon it. He longed to point out that he had built it for his children, who had lived full and rewarding lives in this house. But instead, he bit his tongue and waited for the well man to leave, which he finally did.

Within a day, the Realtor forwarded an offer to him. It was two thousand dollars less than the young couple's offer, and Duane and Sherry promptly rejected it. A counteroffer followed; two thousand dollars better than the couple's offer. They rejected it promptly. Then, there was a request to meet in person. The prospective buyer wanted to discuss the price. Duane and Sherry were inclined to refuse, but the Realtor encouraged them to give it a shot. "People in the real estate business just automatically shoot a lowball offer to start with. Don't be offended; it's just how things work. I think he wants the property, so let's meet with him. You might come to a deal."

The buyer didn't come with an offer of more money; he came with sheet after sheet of deficiencies that his inspector had found. He argued that even at the low price, he could hardly get the building into shape economically because there was just so much wrong with the home. He capped off the argument, saying, "You just won't find another buyer anywhere close to what you are asking."

Normally, Duane and Sherry discuss every major decision in their lives, but one look at Sherry told Duane they didn't need to discuss this one. "That's OK because we are taking the house off the market. We decided to keep it."

Had the conversation ended there, Duane and Sherry would have been irritated at the man sitting across from them, but they became furious when he immediately began offering significantly more money. He had not used the inspection to determine the home's value; he had used it specifically to undermine its worth. As his offers increased, they could tell he never meant to fix any of the deficiencies; he identified them only in an effort to get a better deal for himself.

When he got up to their initial asking price, the Realtor pushed them to accept and pulled out the contract they had signed. He claimed they had to sell it, not realizing Sherry had read the agreement in full. "We withdrew the house from the market ten minutes ago, when the offer on the table was fifteen thousand dollars below our asking price. That means that we only have to pay the withdrawal penalty, and we do not have to sell our house no matter what we are offered."

When the kids heard the news, they were ecstatic. None of them felt they could oppose the sale, but they all wanted to keep their home in the family. They understood that maintenance was an issue, and for a while, they renewed their efforts to come over to the house and help Duane work. He actually enjoyed his projects on the house, and he knew how busy their families were, so he would welcome them whenever they came but was always quick to send them home to keep their own busy schedules. And for the time being, it was no problem, but the whole family knew that someday they would need to decide what to do with the house.

One day, Melissa called Sherry. Obviously excited about something, she invited her mother and father to the farm for lunch. Sherry was inclined to speculate about the surprise, but Duane encouraged her to wait and find out. It didn't stop her.

Fortunately, Missy was as excited to share the news as Sherry was to hear it. They were barely in the house when she asked, "Have you ever watched a program on TV called 'If These Walls Could Talk'?" Duane had watched it once; Sherry had only seen commercials for it.

"Isn't it that history program where they tear apart old buildings looking for stories?"

"And rebuild them," their daughter quickly assured them. "Yeah, that's the program. Anyway, I nominated your house, and they chose it for a program."

"Our house?" protested Sherry, "our house isn't historical."

Sherry explained that she had gone onto the show's website and found out how to nominate a house. Along with pictures of the house and the family, she sent a two-page proposal describing all of the family history built into their home. Apparently, one of the show's producers was interested in the proposal because they had sent a request asking to meet with Duane and Sherry and to take a tour of the house. They explained that if the house was chosen, the show would cover the total cost of renovation and all expenses.

Duane and Sherry quickly realized this would take care of all the maintenance and repairs that had made them think about selling the house, and even though Duane had a strong suspicion of anything "too good to be true," he agreed to meet the producers as requested.

The meeting went well. The producer and his team liked the idea of departing from the formal historical settings and simply documenting a family's personal history as reflected by the family home. The better they got to know Duane and Sherry, the more convinced they were that the show would appeal to their viewers.

They had documented famous sites, filmed gruesome prisons, and ferreted out conspiracies, but they thought their viewers might enjoy an episode about a wholesome family. Partitions built when siblings were feuding, renovations prompted by kids attempting a business, secret passages used to hide dirty laundry when guests were coming to visit; all of these might make an enjoyable series of episodes for their program.

Even Duane began to think it might not be a gimmick. He was prepared to sign the various waivers and releases they had prepared. While Sherry was reading them thoroughly, Duane asked, "So, what's the first step."

"Well, the first thing we will do is send our building inspector to conduct a full inspection of the home…"

———

Duane had almost withdrawn his consent at that moment, but then he realized it wasn't unreasonable for them to want to get an idea of what they were getting into. The logic of the inspection didn't do a lot to change Duane's emotions about the upcoming ordeal. On the day of the scheduled inspection, he had a serious case of butterflies in his stomach.

The Inspector, an elderly gentleman who somehow fitted his picture of a lifetime builder, arrived in a pick-up with a work bed on the back. He hopped out, cheerfully greeted the uncomfortable-looking homeowner, reached out, shook his hand, and cheerfully said, "My name is Brent. Let's get started."

Duane agreed with a distinctly unenthusiastic, "Yes, let's."

Duane had thought the previous two inspectors had been thorough, but they had barely glanced at the house compared to this one. He started on the outside of the house and examined literally every square inch of its exterior. Duane waited to see how he would hide his disapproval, but there was no humming and no "wells." Instead, he looked at each act of creative carpentry with a sincere attempt to understand its purpose.

"I see that you carried the weight of this wall with a beam rather than with what you would more commonly use…"

"It looks like you creatively solved the problem of run-off by…"

But, despite the encouraging comments, Duane still felt the judgment of his workmanship. And some of the comments were much more pointed.

"I'm glad this lasted as long as it did…"

Or,

"I'm glad no one got hurt on this…"

When they moved inside, the feeling only intensified as the inspection became even more painstaking. Brent not only visually inspected the interior but also used a camera equipped with a fiber optic extension to examine the interior of the walls and any void spaces in the construction.

The continuing stream of comments still sounded upbeat, but to Duane, even the comments that affirmed his ingenuity and creativity felt like verbal barbs meant only to make him feel bad. He felt like Brent's only purpose in being there was to belittle him, and he was obviously good at his job. More than once, Duane considered attempting to withdraw from the agreement he had signed. Sherry had advised him that they were past that point, but maybe if he made a big enough stink, this intruder would leave, recommending that the producer cancel the project. Duane would be more than happy to let them cancel the project.

Duane's thoughts were interrupted by another comment from Brent, who was in the basement, standing on a ladder, with his fiber optic lens stuck into a small hole in the ceiling. "It looks like you ran out of floor joists there. Probably not, a great place to make do with whatever was lying around, but it looks like apart from the sheetrock cracking, you've avoided a collapse."

For a moment, Duane's ire was replaced with embarrassment. He knew exactly what Brent was talking about. It had been at the end of a long day. The last thing he wanted was to run into town for a single 2" X 10", so instead of waiting to get one more floor joist, he had patched together the tails he had cut off other boards and scabbed together a filler joist. It was the proper dimension and length but a fraction of the strength. At the time, he had been ashamed of his choice, but rather than rip it out and do it right, he had put down flooring underlayment that night. The next morning, he nailed some OSB to the basement ceiling to hide his workmanship, a step in the building process that had puzzled more than one observer.

The compromise was forgotten until they moved into the house. A squeak quickly developed over the faulty joist. It corresponded to the side of the bed that Sherry usually occupied. The problem was easily remedied. She was more than willing to switch sides of the bed, and at least once every morning since then, Duane had carefully tip-toed out of bed, trying in vain to minimize the creaks underfoot.

To anyone else, he thought he could have admitted the failure, but for this inspector, it was just one more way to run down his hard work, one more fault to add to his list, one more reason to give up.

Then, it occurred to Duane that "giving up" was precisely what he had wished for a minute earlier. Fine, he would admit it. "Yeah, I got lazy that day. I've spent three decades having to tiptoe around it. I'll be glad to have it fixed. But not all of the faults are because of carelessness. It's a good house."

His protest caught Brent's attention. He looked up from the camera screen, and for the first time, Duane met his gaze. He held it for a moment, then said. "I need something at the truck. Why don't you come out with me?"

Duane followed him meekly, expecting to be shown some large book of building codes to prove somehow that Duane had been negligent and ignorant. Instead, when they got to the truck, Brent opened a compartment holding two canvas folding chairs and a lunch box. "It's time for coffee he said, opening the lunch box, "Will you join me? My wife made these."

Duane had to admit that the freshly baked treats looked good, especially since the butterflies had prevented him from eating much breakfast. He agreed and took a chair next to the inspector. The day was beautiful, cool enough for the sunshine to feel good, and by the time Brent had poured him a cup of coffee and handed him a baked treat, Duane was feeling a bit less stressed.

Brent sank back into his chair and enjoyed the sun for a moment, then opened the conversation by asking, "Have you ever had the house inspected before?"

Duane groaned, "Yeah."

"I thought maybe so; tell me about it."

The delicious food, the rich coffee, and the sunshine probably all helped Duane open up. He told about the disappointing outcome of the first inspection and how the buyers just couldn't afford the home. Then, he described how the second buyer used the inspection to undermine its value and how he and Sherry resolved to take the house off the market.

Brent was a thoughtful listener, prompting him with questions until he had the whole picture. Then he posed a question. "Duane, do you know why we conduct an inspection?"

"Well, yeah, I guess so."

"Why do you think we do?" persisted Brent.

"I guess it's so that you can see all of the problems a house has, to see if it's worth your time and money. Why else?"

Brent smiled warmly, "If we had any doubt about this project being worth our resources, I wouldn't even be here. When you accepted our offer, the decision had already been made. They sent me for your sake."

"How nice of them." There was sarcasm, but the bitterness was gone.

"We are undertaking a considerable project. It won't happen quickly, and there will be lots of time for you to wonder what you have gotten yourselves into. Someday, after months of work, you might begin to fear we are thinking about giving up. And then you might remember some of the hidden flaws you know we are about to encounter.

"We need you to know, beyond all doubt, that we will never give up. The only way you can know that is for you to know we will not run into any surprises. We could have plunged into this project confident that once we began, we'd never quit. It would have avoided this inspection and the judgment you are feeling, but it would have cost you the confidence of knowing that nothing we will find here will ever make us give up."

It made sense. Duane had been so happy about the chance to have the house renovated that he had never pictured what it would feel like. The inspection wasn't to determine whether the house was worth the cost; they had already chosen it. The inspection wasn't to devalue the home; they specifically appreciated its uniqueness.

The inspector couldn't help triggering memories of past judgments, but Duane had to admit that the emotional anguish was a small price to pay for the kind of confidence Brent's inspection would give him: Knowing that once they started the project, they would never give up.

Duane looked over at Brent. "Thank You."

"You're welcome. Now, shall we get back to work?"

"I'll hold the ladder."

"Being confident of this one thing,
that he who began a good work in you will
carry it on until it is complete...."

-Paul

Is it possible that the judgment you have felt
As God examines your life,
Isn't the same as the judgment
You have endured from others?

Your new inspector isn't deciding
Whether you are worth the cost,

He is giving you the confidence
That He will never ever give up.

Caleb's Secret

D ylann Teach attended college on an Air Force ROTC (Reserve Officer Training Corp) scholarship. He did well academically, performed all his military training admirably, and was ranked number one at his university and in the top ten percent of all the cadets that year, which is why his ROTC adviser, Major Markson, was so surprised when Teach walked into his office two months before graduation and said, "I quit."

"What?"

"I quit."

Major Markson's military side was overwhelmed by the human side, so instead of a lecture about military courtesy and duty, he simply asked, "Why?"

"I'll never get to fly," answered Teach confidently.

"Why not?"

"My eyes."

"I've seen your records," protested Major Markson, "You have 20/20 vision."

"I do, but flight medical decided that I have to have 20/20 vision—correctable," explained Dylann.

"What's the difference?" asked the major, who usually dispenses information to the cadets rather than requests it.

"As part of my flight physical, they put something in my eye to totally relax it before taking measurements of my eyes, and they determined that I need glasses. So, even though I don't need glasses to pass the test, I now have to wear glasses when I take the test, and when I wear glasses, I can't pass the depth perception part of the test. Glasses mess me up, Sir," explained Teach, finally remembering his Military courtesy.

"That sounds totally stupid and just like something the Air Force would do," commented Markson, indulging in a rare expression of frustration, which he seldom did in front of the trainees, "but there are other jobs…"

"I love planes, Sir," replied Teach.

Major Markson's military sensibilities gradually caught up after Dylann's surprise announcement: "It doesn't matter what you want. You can't just walk out after the Air Force has invested so much in you. You would have to pay back your tuition."

"Or…?" prompted Dylann, knowing the answer.

"…Or you would have to serve enlisted,"

Dylann nodded, which puzzled Major Markson even more. "You want to be enlisted instead of commissioned? It's quite a pay cut, and you still wouldn't be flying. I don't get it, Teach."

"I love planes, Sir. If I can't fly them, I want to fix them, and the Air Force doesn't let officers repair planes. If I got commissioned, they might put me in charge of a maintenance unit, but I'll never get to work on planes personally," explained Dylann. Although it definitely wasn't the last time they discussed it, Dylann Teach signed the paperwork refusing his commission and enlisted in the Air Force.

With his engineering training, Dylann excelled at his tech school, and once he was assigned to his duty station, he was quickly recognized as one of the best mechanics in his squadron. On evenings and weekends, while the other airmen were killing Zombies on their computers or barhopping in town, Dylann would sit in his room reading the manuals and bulletins he had borrowed from the maintenance squadron's informal library.

Soon, he was moved from regular maintenance to diagnosing problems. The civilian contractors with whom he worked quickly recognized his competence. As he neared the end of his enlistment, they tempted him to come and work as a contractor with offers of money, but Dylann liked the Air Force. He had married his longtime girlfriend Darla, who was enjoying the social life she shared with the other Air Force spouses living in their housing area.

The other thing Dylann liked about the Air Force was his schedule. As long as his work was finished, he could use the rest of his time as he chose. His amusement of choice was working on more airplanes. After completion of his Air Force training, it had only taken Dylann a few extra months to study for and pass the exam for his civilian A&P (Airframe and Powerplant) certificate. This meant he was qualified to work on civilian airplanes.

The world of private aviation probably has more addicts than any other segment of society. Not drug addicts, but people who otherwise appear responsible, who will do anything they can to get up in a plane. And the thing you need most to fly is not a plane; it is money. Even once you own a plane, the costs keep mounting. Maintenance is costly, especially if the plane is just for personal enjoyment. The schedule for airplane maintenance is very rigid. Inspections must be conducted precisely at the correct time, and all repairs must be completed by a certified mechanic.

All of this was perfect for Dylann. He found plenty of amateur pilots who would happily trade him flight time for his maintenance services. Dylann, without the Air Force's strict eye rules, finally had the opportunity to fly. Soon, he had his private license, and after that, most license upgrades require a little study and a lot of flight hours.

Dylann began adding a variety of ratings to his license. He was certified for commercial flight, flight instruction, pontoon landings, ski landings, single and multiple engines, skydiving flights, and any other qualifications for which he could find a qualified instructor to teach him and sign off.

He enjoyed both his Air Force work and his sideline employment, but he loved flying. Darla started to resent time-sharing her husband with the sky until he began taking her along on flights. She found that she enjoyed the sky, too, and soon, she had her private license and was working on all her personal upgrades.

So they worked and flew their way through Dylann's Air Force career until just a few years remained until his retirement. The couple often discussed the changes that would bring. They would miss the full Air Force paycheck, but the military pension would cover a significant portion of the monthly bills. Dylann figured he could make enough money doing mechanic work to keep comfortable, but Darla longed to do something exciting and adventurous with their retirement. She knew they didn't have enough money to fly around the world, but she wanted them to do something interesting with the freedom retirement would offer.

Seventeen years into his enlistment, the Department of the Air Force realized that Master Sergeant Teach had managed to make himself so useful that he had avoided many of the transfers which make up normal Air Force life. Most airmen are unsure why the

Department of the Air Force insists on shuffling people around, but the personnel managers weren't about to start a new precedent with Teach, so he came down on orders for Eielson Air Force Base near Fairbanks, Alaska.

The news came as a surprise to Dylann, but it was almost a relief to Darla. Moving was a hassle, but she was ready for something new. Once Dylann had accepted that none of the officers on base, who owed him favors, could get the orders changed, he suggested to his wife that they request a week of leave and take a commercial flight up to Fairbanks and check things out.

Landing at the airport, Dylann fell in love with Alaska. There were planes everywhere.

Typically, an airport will be divided between the commercial side and the general aviation side. In most large airports, the bulk of the activity is on the commercial side. The airport in Fairbanks breaks from that norm. Dylann was glued to his window as they landed, gawking at the impressive collection of aircraft lined up on the general aviation side. Some were planes so old they belonged in a museum, except they were obviously still in active service. Others were experimental aircraft, which he had never seen but about which he had read. There was even a landing pond for float planes.

Once they had moved to Alaska, it took Dylann little time to connect with the civilian flying community in and around Fairbanks. Plenty of pilots were happy to trade flying time for maintenance work, and most weekends, Darla and Dylann would be out exploring their new surroundings from the air.

Within six months, Dylann was a fixture in the aviation community, and many pilots recognized that he was probably the best mechanic around when it came to figuring out a mechanical mystery.

One day, he got a call from one of his customers. After exchanging greetings, the amateur pilot got right to the point.

"Dylann, something's wrong with my plane. I don't know what, but I had to leave it out in the bush. The local mechanic couldn't figure out what was wrong. Will you take a flight out, see if you can fix it, and fly it home? I'll pay all expenses."

"The bush" meant that the plane was trapped in a part of the state unreachable by the limited road system. Dylann would have to take along everything he might need when he flew out to the village where the plane was stranded, but a few questions convinced him that he knew what was wrong with the aircraft, so he agreed to take the job.

The flight out was more pleasant than he expected. As a pilot, he always felt uncomfortable when he wasn't the one flying the plane, but the regional airline on which his friend had booked the ticket seemed professionally run. Getting on the plane, however, was a little like crashing a family reunion. Everybody knew everyone else, and as the small plane filled, everybody began talking about their experiences on their visit to Fairbanks. Their excitement was contagious, and soon, Dylann was invited into their conversations. Everyone wanted to know everything about his reason for visiting their village, which they were very proud of.

Throughout the uneventful flight, Dylann began to feel a bond with the residents of the small village. He began to understand the challenges they faced living so far removed from the rest of the world. One of the complaints, to which they often returned, was the one freshest in their minds: the cost of airline tickets. For those who didn't have their own plane, traveling to Fairbanks or Anchorage meant chartering a plane or buying a ticket from the regional airline, and it seemed like the regional airline knew they had a captive audience.

As the plane approached the tiny airfield, Dylann was struck by how desolate the village appeared. A few miles to the west, one could catch sight of the ocean, but the settlement itself was located inland along the mouth of a river. Topographically, the area was quite plain, and it looked as if a big wave could wash in from the ocean with nothing to stop it but some scrub bushes growing out of the muskeg. This outpost of humanity certainly had nothing to commend itself to the outsider, but despite its barrenness, Dylann enjoyed his stay. Fifteen minutes after he had arrived, the whole population seemed to know who he was, and several folks stopped by to offer assistance while he worked on his friend's plane.

The repairs went as scheduled, so the next day, Dylann left his new "home away from home." As he looked back to see the village fading in the distance, he felt an interesting bond with the tiny town and its people, and with it, an idea began to grow.

On the next free weekend, Dylann invited Darla to take a flight with him in a plane on which he had performed a scheduled inspection in trade for flight time. They left early Saturday morning and flew out to the village. Dylann landed in the desolate-looking town, suggesting to his wife that they get something to eat there before the long flight back. He explained, "This was where I went to fix that plane a few weeks ago; I thought you might like to see the place."

"There's not much to see," she thought to herself. But she answered, "It'll feel good to stretch the legs."

Walking up the short main street to the only cafe, Darla was struck by how many people Dylann knew. "You were only here a day. Do you know everyone?"

"Just about," he guessed. "Friendly, aren't they?"

She had to agree, if not then, certainly by the time they had finished lunch, and another dozen people stopped by to greet Dylann like a long-lost friend. They received two offers for a place to sleep if they wanted to stay the night and an invitation to return in two weeks for the volunteer fire department supper, one of the few big events in the village.

Dylann could tell Darla was impressed with the friendliness of the residents, so on his way back, he brought up his new idea to her: "How would you like living there?"

"It might be fun," she admitted, "But what would you do?" She queried.

"I was thinking of starting an airline."

———

During the long flight home in the borrowed plane, they discussed the idea from every possible angle. It would cost more than Dylann's retirement to live out there in the bush, but he could probably earn a living doing what he loved most: flying. Most of their musings led to questions which couldn't be answered any other way than by trying it. Driving home from the airfield, Darla gave her final approval: "I think we should go for it."

She was more than convinced that she had made the right choice when they returned to the village for a town meeting about the proposed air service. The citizens, desperate for affordable transportation, treated them like heroes.

While in the village, Dylann also found a good lead on an airplane. One of the residents took him to a weather-worn hanger on the end of the airfield. They didn't have a key, but Dylann caught a glimpse of a twin-engine aircraft through the dirty window. He easily recognized the Beechcraft Model 18, known as a Twin Beech. His guide explained that the plane had been sitting there for ten years since the pilot who owned it had suffered a heart attack and subsequently died. "No one has ever flown it since then. His wife is getting old, but she won't leave. She wants to die here, too. And she can't bear the thought of selling her husband's plane, but you could ask," offered the helpful villager.

Dylann was already making a mental tally of all of the maintenance and inspections the venerable old airplane would require. It would be prohibitive if you had to hire professional mechanics, but since he could do the work himself, it might mean that he could afford the plane. Capable of hauling 10 passengers, it would be the perfect plane for his plan to provide economical air service to the village.

The next morning, before he and Darla left, they walked to the edge of town to the small house a neighbor indicated was the home of the plane's owner. They knocked on the door. A small woman in her eighties answered the door. She kept her cozy cottage in perfect order and seemed pleased to have company.

"Come on in," she invited. "My name is Connie; you must be the couple who want to ask about the plane."

Dylann should have known that she would have heard the purpose of his visit before he arrived. The village didn't seem to keep secrets very well. "That's right, I am Dylann Teach, and this is my wife Darla." They shook hands, and she led them to the kitchen, seated them at her table, and got coffee. Sharing a cup of coffee was part of the cost of doing business with her.

"Now about the plane…" she said, introducing the topic.

"Yes, well, I am looking for a plane to start an air service," Dylann began.

"Yep, I know all about that. Do you think you can do it?"

"I sure want to try. But I don't have a lot of money. I thought maybe I could afford your husband's old plane because, as a mechanic, I could repair it myself." Then, realizing it sounded like he was trying to chisel the price, he tried to explain. "You see, no matter what the condition the plane was in when it was parked, now that it has sat unused, it will need to be completely redone."

"Oh yes, I know about that, and more than one person who wanted to buy it explained the same thing. I don't need the plane, obviously, but I don't need the money either. So it comes down to this: there are few things I would like better than hearing Ray's plane flying overhead, I could always tell which plane was his, and I'll bet I still can. Everyone who has made an offer on the plane was going to take it away, but if you promise to keep the plane flying around here, I'll sell."

Dylann looked at Darla with an anxious smile. "I can't promise I'll be able to make a go of the air service, but I'll promise to do my best."

"That's a good enough promise for me." Then Connie switched from her grandmother voice to her business tone. "The book value of an operating Twin beech is fairly well established, so what if we look that up and set it as the base price, minus parts and all of your hours fixing it? Half to be paid when you get it flying, and half to be paid after your first year in business."

Dylann's smile wasn't tentative now; he was delighted.

Over the next six months, any time he wasn't at work, he was either earning flight time by working on planes or he was in the village working on "his" plane.

He flew it for the first time two months before his scheduled retirement. Plans were underway to pack and ship their household to the little house they were going to rent in the village, and Dylann was kept busy with all of the various out-processing appointments the Air Force insisted were needed.

It was only a month before he hoped to start flying when he finally got around to setting up the business side of his airline. He hired an attorney to set up the business. Mostly, it was just a matter of filing paperwork, but it was the attorney who informed him of the requirement that he be bonded. Dylann hadn't given much thought to the idea of insurance. He knew that liability was a problem, but he was convinced that the best way to avoid such problems was to not be insured. It is much easier for a plaintiff to get a settlement if insurance is conveniently in place. If he had no insurance, a judgment might take his business, but with no debt, he could afford to lose it. However, he hoped that the biggest disincentive for a lawyer not to file suit against him would be the revelation that there was no easy money to be had.

His attorney agreed in principle, but this was a legal requirement. He recommended an agent who specialized in aviation insurance, so Dylann reluctantly went to meet him.

The agent had retired from the Air Force, and he and Dylann quickly developed that connection, comparing notes on various places they had served, and people they had both known. But when the insurance question came up, he had no good news for Dylann. The price of the basic coverage would almost double the operating costs Dylann had budgeted. He would have to charge more for the tickets to make up the difference.

"Isn't there anything cheaper?" he pleaded.

The agent began checking with other providers to see what factors might reduce the cost of insurance. "Here's something that costs about a fourth as much." He commented.

"Really?" asked Dylann, his hopes rising.

"Oh, that's why?"

"What?"

"That price is for a skydiving service," the agent explained.

"Why is that so much cheaper?" questioned Dylann.

"I guess it is because everybody is wearing a parachute and already planning to jump out." He focused on his computer again, searching for a competitive price, but Dylann was lost in thought.

A few minutes later, Dylann asked, "What if a passenger changes his mind?"

"Pardon me?" said the agent, obviously having lost Dylann's train of thought.

"What if a skydiver chickens out?"

"I suppose they would land with the pilot," the agent guessed, not seeing where the question was headed.

"Would the pilot have to land at the same airport?"

"I can check, but I doubt there is any restriction on where you would land," the insurance man surmised.

"Then I'm going to start a skydiving service," concluded Dylann

"Where? In the village? I can't imagine much demand for skydiving in the bush."

Dylann got a smug smile, "Can I help it if all my passengers change their mind?"

On his next visit to the village, he explained the loophole to the residents. They didn't seem to mind that they would have to wear a parachute for each flight. It was worth it if Dylann could keep the price low. But some of the more practically-minded passengers asked, "Where will we get parachutes?"

"Honestly, I haven't really figured that out, but I imagine I will have a set with the plane for customers to use," temporized Dylann. "I'll let you know."

When Dylann began searching for parachutes, he found another obstacle awaiting him. The price of a parachute was reasonable compared to the cost of a ticket. Dylann figured customers would save the upfront cost of the parachute by the fourth ticket they bought, but what wasn't cheap was getting them packed and certified. Dylann had assumed that he could hand each passenger a parachute for the duration of the flight. He discovered that each time a parachute was assigned to a new customer, a full inspection was required, whether or not anyone had used it. The cost of recertification would wipe out any savings he hoped to get by being a skydiving service. Plus, owning the parachutes hiked his liability insurance back up, Unless...

Dylann called one of his friends from the village and explained the predicament. The only way they could keep the airline inexpensive was to have the passengers purchase their own parachute. It would be a one-time cost upfront, but as long as the parachutes never changed hands, they wouldn't have to get inspected. Dylann offered to carry a line of parachutes for people to purchase and the residents readily agreed to this unorthodox way to save money.

It was definitely unusual, but it worked out just fine. As the passengers lined up to board their flight, Dylann would inspect each parachute's certificate. Once he checked them off his manifest, they would board the plane. When the plane was safely in the air, Dylann would ask them, "Anybody feel like jumping today?" Then, they would proceed to Fairbanks on Mondays and Thursdays and Anchorage on Tuesdays and Fridays.

Most passengers quickly got used to the new arrangement, which was a minor inconvenience in exchange for affordable flights. The regional carrier responded by dropping its service rather than trying to undercut Dylann.

There were, however, some passengers who never felt comfortable with the question waiting for them in the air. Adam had grown up in the village, and whenever he heard the question, he wanted to say, "Yes!" He longed to jump out of the plane. Any time he met someone who had been skydiving or who had been a paratrooper in the military, he would ask them what it was like. The more stories he heard, the more he wanted to see what it was like for himself. He didn't want to play it safe; he wanted to put his parachute to the test.

Brett also could not get used to the standard question, but for him, the question was surrounded in fear. When Dylann asked if anyone wanted to jump, Brett pictured himself standing at the open door, staring into the void. He would wake up with nightmares of having to jump out of a plane. If only Dylann wouldn't mention it. He thought he could ignore his fears if "The Question" wasn't always waiting to remind him. But he needed to make the journey to Fairbanks at least once a month for his work, so now, with the commercial air carrier gone, he had no choice but to fly on Dylann's skydiving service. On the flight, he would wear his earbuds and turn up his music as loud as he could, but he could not ignore the moment when Dylann asked "The Question."

One day, Adam approached him with a proposition. "How would you like to go skydiving with me?"

Brett was speechless, struggling to overcome the anxiety the question produced and trying to put into words how little he would like that. But Adam took his silence as indecision and continued trying to sell him on the idea.

"You see, every time Dylann asks us if anyone wants to jump, I have always thought I would. I want to feel what it's like to fall through the air, totally supported by something I couldn't see. Dylann told me he would take us up if I could find someone to jump with me."

"You can count me out. I can't imagine not being terrified of trusting what you can't see. I guess I'm just wired that way," Brett concluded, trying to politely dismiss the subject.

"I guess so," agreed Adam. "I'm a little afraid, but still, I think it's worth getting over."

"Getting over what?"

"My fear."

"I don't think that's possible," asserted Brett. I've tried everything I could to overcome or ignore the fear."

"Have you told anyone." queried Adam.

"Just you, now."

"Well, maybe you need help."

"I doubt it," countered Brett.

It took Adam three months to convince his friend to go skydiving. They had talked it over repeatedly, and even though

Brett was still scared, he realized that once he had admitted his fears, the terror had diminished... slightly. It had transformed from a vague and debilitating fear into a rational proposition. "Could he make the leap?" He understood the theory, the history, and the advantages of a parachute. Still, jumping was the only way to convince himself to trust the parachute.

He might never need to jump. Most people boarded the plane, never thinking that the parachute was anything more than a formality, and maybe they were right. But what if they did need to jump? He wasn't willing to face that danger with an untested faith in parachutes.

Brett finally agreed, and Adam set up a date for the jump before his friend could lose his nerve. Dylann had found that a WWII airfield seven miles inland was still serviceable. It made a perfect landing zone, and after the drop, he could land, pick up the skydivers, and bring them back to town.

To Brett's credit, they didn't have to physically throw him out of the plane, and once he was sitting on the ground at the abandoned airfield waiting for Dylann to land and pick them up, Brett was finally able to admit he was glad he had made the jump. He trusted his parachute. Every chance Adam got, he would go skydiving, and sometimes Brett would go with him. Over time, others joined the little group for whom Dylann's Skydiving Service was more than just an economic loophole. Most of the villagers thought some mental aberration drove these mavericks to risk their lives for no good purpose. As one respected elder put it, "They must be crazy." But for them, jumping was a dynamic part of their life. It was sometimes frustrating for these adventurous souls to realize that they lived in a town where everyone owned a parachute, but so few actually dared to jump.

Almost everyone owned a parachute.

Caleb had recently moved to the village. He came for work reasons and, by and large, he disliked the place. It wasn't the desolate landscape, the cold winters, or the months of darkness that bothered him. He didn't like the community, or maybe it was more accurate to say that he couldn't like the community. Something early in Caleb's life, or in his emotional makeup, had convinced him that everyone was out to get him. Not physically, but financially. In his mind, everything was a scam, and his central purpose had become not to let himself be taken in. In normal society, it might have been a useful guard, even though it was often a social liability. Here in the village, people tended to cooperate and help one another out of a sense of unity emerging from the challenge of facing unforgiving weather and prolonged isolation. This left Caleb constantly confused. No one was out to get him or his money. Instead of changing his outlook on life, he searched harder for the scam, continually imagining nonexistent selfish motives.

The result was that the warm welcome Dylann and Darla had felt couldn't penetrate Caleb's defenses. The challenges of life in the village were quickly compounded by the social isolation that his constant suspicion created. The by-product of this isolation was a malady called "cabin fever," which many people in the village, in addition to Caleb, contracted. The accepted remedy was a trip to town. Either destination, Fairbanks or Anchorage, would do, but sometimes a person needed to be tangibly reminded that the world is a bigger place than one dirty main street through a collection of wind-battered houses.

Occasionally, Caleb's employer would send a plane for him when his official duties required his presence back in the civilized world, but eventually, Caleb asked one of his acquaintances about getting a flight out of the village. The long-time resident directed him to the skydiving service, praising the inexpensive flights and explaining the need to purchase a parachute if he wanted to travel by that means.

Immediately, Caleb smelled a rat. Somebody was up to something, and he wasn't about to let them take advantage of him. Fortunately, it was easy to see through this one.

"So, where do I get a parachute? I suppose the skydiving service sells them," Caleb asked, barely keeping a sneer out of his voice.

The villager confirmed this and assured Caleb that the cost of a parachute was relatively low compared to what flights used to cost.

Convinced that this was just another scam, he refused to even talk to Dylann or Darla. But as the months dragged on and cabin fever intensified, Caleb decided that even if he couldn't avoid doing business with them, he could at least break their parachute monopoly. He got online and went to Ebay. Entering "parachute" in the search box resulted in hundreds of pages of options. He knew that he didn't really understand what he was looking for. The jargon of skydiving was like a foreign language to him, but he had discovered one of the practical ways of learning was to read about the products. Some eBay sellers are good about giving a complete tutorial on their product's use.

Caleb was on page three when he saw a listing;

Parachute pack $5
ATTENTION! DOES NOT INCLUDE PARACHUTE!"

Caleb clicked anyway, and a plan began to form in his mind. He didn't really need the parachute. With no plans to jump, he just needed to satisfy their little scam. This was a perfect solution. He placed a bid on the parachute pack and won the auction for $15.37 plus $5.89 shipping. He had what he needed to fly.

He got the pack a week or so later. An old bedsheet was folded, taking about the same volume as a tightly packed chute. He stuffed it into the pack and felt the exterior. It looked and felt just right.

No one would know it was a sham. He had studied more while waiting for the pack to arrive and had a pretty good idea of how to forge the certification papers. After scribbling an unreadable signature in a couple of boxes, he was ready to take his parachute on a test run. The day came for his flight, and he lined up at Dylann's hanger. He had purchased a ticket from Darla, telling her he already owned a parachute. As the last hurdle before loading the plane, Dylann walked down the line and checked each of his passenger's parachutes. He spent a moment longer on Caleb's pack because he had never seen it before, but the certification with its illegible scrawls seemed valid, so Dylann checked him off on his paperwork.

Caleb's smug grin didn't wear off until he was halfway to Anchorage. His parachute worked just fine, and now that he had passed the first inspection, he knew that future checks would be merely perfunctory. He had beat the scam.

So life continued much the same. Dylann's skydiving service became a regular part of village life. Adam and Brett, with a few of their friends, kept insisting on jumping, but the rest of the population kept their chutes, never really expecting to use them. And Caleb kept his secret.

One night in late October, Dylann and Darla were awakened at two o'clock in the morning by a pounding on their door. When they opened the door, an older gentleman stood in the porch light. Dylann knew him well; he was the commander of the local Civil Air Patrol (CAP)

CAP, an auxiliary of the Air Force, organizes aviation enthusiasts to assist communities and emergency services in times of need. The village had a fairly active chapter, and Dylann himself was a member, attending meetings whenever possible.

The commander stepped in and told Dylann and Darla to get dressed and come to his office as soon as possible. Dylann was inclined to ask why, but he could see the intensity on the commander's face.

They pulled up to the office in about seven minutes, and when Dylann and Darla walked into the conference room, the commander said, "Good, you are here. I'll start the brief,"

Looking at his watch, he said, "Three and a half hours ago, there was an underwater earthquake off the Kamchatka Peninsula. The quake registered higher than any recent quake. What that means to us is that we have a Tsunami headed this way. The best estimates are that the whole village will be flooded by the initial wave, and there is a suspicion that the wave will block the river, resulting in secondary flooding. There is no way to tell how deep the water will get here, but it seems clear that we have to evacuate.

The room began to buzz until the commander called for attention again. "We have a request pending for a Coast Guard C-130, but it has been tasked to other communities. They passed on the request for an Air Force bird out of Eielson, but it looks like it may not get here on time. I am not in favor of waiting and hoping. Does anyone want to take that chance?" He scanned the room, looking for objections and finding none. "Right, then, let's figure out how to get our people out of here."

They immediately sent some CAP volunteers to begin waking up the rest of the villagers. "Tell them they can each take one small bag. That's it. We need them here to start flying out in half an hour. No longer."

The other local pilots were already gathering and listing the number of passengers they could transport. But even with every plane full, a significant number of villagers still needed a ride. The commander turned to Dylann, "We need you to take multiple loads."

"OK, I don't have anything else on my schedule tonight, but I don't see how I can possibly get more than two, possibly three, loads before the wave hits. A round trip to the closest airport inland takes way too long."

"I know," said the commander, "and we probably need seven loads. What about your abandoned landing strip?"

Dylann did a quick calculation in his mind. With a few minutes to load and refuel, he still didn't think he could fit seven trips to the abandoned airfield before the wave was scheduled to hit.

"It's still too tight," Dylann protested.

"I'm ahead of you on that," agreed the commander. "But…"

"But what?" Dylann could tell he had an idea, "What are you thinking?"

"Well, we've all been carrying these parachutes around just in case. I think this is the case."

Once he had dropped them at the airfield, the Air Force C-130 could pick them up whenever it got there. Dylann walked to the area map on the wall and checked the altitude of the old landing strip. It should be high enough so that the tsunami wouldn't reach it. With a hundred contingencies running through his mind, he turned to the commander and said, "All right. Get these other planes on their way, and we will start ferrying out the rest."

Within minutes, most of the villagers started gathering. The personally owned aircraft were lined up ready for takeoff, and anybody who couldn't make the parachute jump—kids, the disabled, and the elderly—was loaded up, and the planes headed for civilization.

Everyone else was going to make the jump. Suddenly, Caleb realized that he had a problem. He needed a parachute. He would have to humble himself and admit that he had been lying, but what other choice did he have? He walked over to where Darla was standing at the skydiving office. He figured that maybe in the bustle of the night, he could quietly buy a new parachute from her, and no one would notice. Still, something in Caleb hated to admit his secret. He had been so proud of how he outsmarted them, and now they would have the last laugh. Not the way he wanted it to go, but what could he do? As he was walking towards the office, he heard a commotion. In all the excitement, someone had backed up their vehicle without watching where they were going and had run over the foot and ankle of one of the villagers named Sam, who had been standing nearby.

The driver felt horrible and profusely apologized as he realized that the injury might affect the parachute jump. Darla ran over to see what had happened, and Caleb followed, needing desperately to get a hold of Darla and buy a parachute.

As he approached the crowd, he heard Darla's verdict. "It will be OK," she assured the driver. We will take Sam out on the last flight. He won't have to jump. He can land with us in the plane and be all right."

That was it—salvation for Caleb. He wouldn't have to admit his deception; he could just wait for the last flight, and he would be OK.

Then it was discovered that not only had the vehicle crushed Sam's ankle, it had run into a pile of luggage, including Sam's wife Caren's parachute. There was a long tear in the covering, which obviously went through the fabric of the outer layer and into the parachute material. She held up the damaged chute for Darla to see. Darla, reacting quickly, pulled out her keys and sent Caren to the office. "There is one parachute left in the storage room."

Careen took off towards the hanger, and the collected crowd breathed a sigh of relief. On a night of seemingly unnumbered crisis, another one had been averted.

Some people faced that night in a haze of unbelief; the whole situation seemed surreal. Others found the ability to assimilate all of the challenges and step forward with the strength to lead others. Adam was one of these leaders. He had quickly organized each of his friends who had jumped previously as leaders of a flight. These experienced skydivers carefully inspected each jumper's equipment, making suggestions to keep them safe and offering encouragement to those who were apprehensive.

Some villagers were more than apprehensive; they were terrified. To these, Brett was a godsend. More than once, he told them stories about how frightened he had been. When they could laugh about his fears, it helped them put their own fears in perspective. Admittedly, his flight was filled with a disproportionate number of these frightened jumpers, but in the end, he helped them all safely out of the plane and to the ground.

But the real surprise was how helpful Caleb was. He seemed to be everywhere helping others, loading their gear, and running last-minute errands. Each time he was scheduled for a flight, he would graciously offer to wait and let others go first. The change in his behavior surprised most people, who had always found him suspicious and a bit distant. Moments of need sometimes bring out the best in people; apparently, Caleb was like that.

Then, with two flights to go, something happened. Suddenly, at the end of the runway, a large four-wheel-drive, four-door pick-up appeared speeding across the open ground from the opposite direction of the village.

The few remaining passengers were surprised, thinking they were the area's last residents. What they had forgotten was the fishing settlement down the coast. It wasn't technically connected by a road, but a serious off-road vehicle could make the trip in a pinch. The villagers had been too busy with their own evacuation to check with their closest neighbors. But now, there was at least one more passenger for the flight. And just in time. It appeared that the last flight would get away only minutes before the wave hit.

All four truck doors opened simultaneously, and fourteen children of all ages, including the driver, poured out of the cab and off the bed. Immediately, Darla understood the new challenge. Their neighboring village had sent their children to safety when they discovered they might not be picked up in time. The adults would fare the wave or the flooding the best they could, but they hoped the children would be taken to safety.

Darla called the children over to an ancient meat scale that had been brought to the airfield for the evacuation. Darla began calculating the total weight of all the children. The remaining passengers drew closer, waiting for her determination.

She looked up and saw everyone gathered around. "Weight-wise, we can make it," she announced. The kids will all go out on the last flight. Sam, you will ride in the co-pilot seat. But nothing else will fit."

She was interrupted by the sound of Dylann's returning plane. "I'll take this flight," she said, reaching for her parachute. "We'll give Sam's parachute to the driver. Caleb, thanks for all your help, but this will be your flight, too."

Suddenly, Caleb realized that no matter what he had planned, how smart he thought he was, or who he had fooled, he had no parachute for the jump.

"For it is appointed unto a man once to die,
and after that to face the judgment."

-Paul

Your parachute pack may look full to others,
but people's approval doesn't really matter.
Are you willing to trust it with your life?

Is there any way, like Adam or Brett, that you
could test your faith before the final jump?
If so, are you willing to do it,
even if people think you are crazy?

Trixie

Katrina, who had the nickname Kat, was eight years old, and more than anything else Kat wanted a dog. She couldn't comprehend how her parents had never noticed that fact because almost everything she did was intended as a hint. Whenever she had to draw something in art class she drew a picture of a little girl with her own dog. Whenever she had to write a story, she always wrote about a little girl with her very own dog. Whenever she needed to write a report for science, she would research dogs. Only math class seemed impervious to dog hints until the teacher assigned the students to accompany their parents on a shopping trip and write down the prices of their favorite products. Kat made a beeline to the dog food aisle.

As you might guess her parents had not missed the recurring theme, they had thoroughly discussed the possibility of a dog. And Dad had been very clear about the role of a pet. He wanted Kat to have a dog, but not until she was old enough to take genuine responsibility for the pet. Few things irritated Dad more than people who would, on the spur of the moment, give in to their child's begging and purchase a pet, choosing to ignore the fact that likely, in a very short amount of time, it would be merely tolerated by its family as a pest which they were now obligated to put up with for the rest of its life. Dad believed that a dog could tell, and cared enough about animals to make sure that they wouldn't get a pet until Kat could consistently work with it and train it to fit into the dynamic of their family.

Mom knew that if Kat did lose interest in the dog, much of the burden would fall to her, and so even though she was tempted to give into her daughter's elaborate hinting, she knew her husband was right, pets were about the worst thing you could get for a kid, if they weren't ready.

Stan Colby had recently discovered that truth. Stan was the owner of a series of businesses in a city several hundred miles from where Kat and her family lived. Stan was proud of those businesses, or was at least proud of the money they made. If he ever gave it some thought, he might have realized he was deeply ashamed of the businesses. They were an eclectic conglomerate, and the only thing they had in common was Stan, the owner, and the fact that they all were mildly immoral. None were technically illegal. He had begun by purchasing a string of convenience stores which, in the days before the internet, brought adult magazines into small communities. In several communities, the move had been heralded with a measure of outrage. But he guessed rightly that the majority of customers would slowly come to accept the lowered moral standard.

That business had been followed by a string of others catering to the basest appetites of the public, or in some other way pushing the limits of ethical business. Stan didn't care as long as he made money. Money made him somebody, and the more he had, the more he acted out his belief that fiscal net worth gave him a pass to do what he pleased.

After just a few years it cost him his marriage; when he found out that while he had enough money to attract women who otherwise might have been turned off by his boorish behavior, he did not have enough money to convince his wife to ignore his philandering. He had purchased a more expensive lawyer than his wife could afford and managed to get through the divorce without losing everything. He chalked the win up to his legal strategy and his careful screens for his hidden assets; never realizing that his ex accepted such a small settlement because she just wanted him out of her life.

They had a daughter from their time together, and Stan, emboldened by his legal victory, maneuvered for a significant custody role. He hoped to diminish his child support burden, even though his daughter was practically a stranger to him. Again, his wife did not fight visitation as vigorously as she wanted to, because she hoped that at least he might build a relationship with their daughter.

He dreaded those visits. To him, they were merely an interruption to his new bachelor social life, and he lacked the maturity to relate to the young lady his daughter was becoming. So, he fell back on his money and began buying her things. Each visit he would have some new and more expensive stuff waiting for her, and she quickly learned that if she could show only tepid enthusiasm for the gift, then, on the next visit he would have something more expensive waiting to try to buy her vote in the "who's the best parent" poll, which he was constantly running.

He had pretty much used up the toys and electronics categories when in response to her begging, he bought her a puppy. He hadn't thought the purchase through, past the scene where she hugged him and said, "You're the best Dad in the whole world!" And he hadn't checked with his ex-wife.

To her it was simple.

"She can most certainly have a puppy, which she will get to visit whenever she visits your house."

Stan had even gone as far as offering to pay her to keep the dog, but his Ex remained firm. So he had a new roommate. Everyone who saw the puppy remarked how cute it was, but to Stan, it was a non-stop source of irritation which he could never get rid of, because his daughter, even though she seldom played with it, refused to let him give it away.

The staff at his main office, mostly glamorous women without enough self-respect to find a less demeaning boss, were daily treated to his complaints about the puppy. One day after his diatribe, one of the newer secretaries asked him to bring the dog in for them to see and, since he had more than a business interest in her, he complied. The puppy was a big hit. All the ladies loved the cute ball of fluff, despite his complaints. The only one who shared Stan's opinion was his chief of staff; a college friend and a father who had children of his own, as well as a badly behaved family pet which he had bought for his kids in what he called "a moment of temporary insanity."

He commiserated with his boss, "God must have hated dads when he made puppies so cute. Even if you do train them, by the time you can stand them they aren't cute anymore. Whoever finds out how to sell a dog as cute as a puppy and as well trained as a grown dog will make a million."

The metaphorical light bulb lit up for Stan. Leaving the puppy for the secretaries to watch he invited his chief of staff into his office. Turning to the surprised assistant he stated, "We are going to do that."

"Do what?"

"We are going to sell perfectly trained puppies," asserted Stan.

"You can't even train one puppy, why would you think that you could produce trained dogs when no one else can?"

"Because most people who train dogs don't hate them as much as I do."

Under Stan's direction, it took surprisingly little time to establish a kennel. He transferred two employees whom he was confident he could trust for the project, and they set up a training arena in a rented building. The sides of the arena were lined with cages where they kept any and every cheap puppy they could find. Few were anything more than mutts, but Stan didn't care. Every day at feeding time the trainers brought in a well-trained older dog. They would have the dog perform a trick and give the dog a bite of food. Then, they would go around to each of the cages and give the puppies a chance to perform the same trick. Only the dogs who could perform got fed. The others got hungry.

The dogs that could do the tricks got food each day and had their behaviors reinforced, The dogs that couldn't, got hungrier until they learned or died.

Meanwhile, Kat had adjusted her strategy a little. She had discovered that her grandparents responded much more positively to her pictures and stories featuring her with a dog. She redirected her hinting to where she thought it would do some good. Kat's mother's parents lived closest to them, and even though they had a hard time resisting Kat's hinting, they respected their son-in-law enough not to contradict his decision. Then, one day, Grandpa was dragged to the mall to shop with Grandma. He performed this task by finding the nearest bench and informing her, "I'll be right here if you need me."

On this particular day, his bench was in front of the pet store. The display window was a popular attraction for shoppers, and Grandpa actually enjoyed watching the shoppers, their children, and the pets. While he sat there, he watched as a puppy was brought out for a demonstration. Several minutes into the show, Grandpa had stood up and joined the crowd.

A little puppy who hardly seemed old enough to be away from its mother was performing an amazing litany of tricks: beg, roll-over, play dead, heel, kennel up, dance, and shake, one after the other, with just a brief pause between each trick for a treat. Grandma came and joined the show, sharing the crowd's amazement at the little puppy. Like a skeptic at a magic show, one of the observers tried to figure out if there was a catch.

"What if I pick the puppy?"

The clerk assured him that all the dogs were equally well trained, and let the doubter pick the next puppy for the demonstration.

The next afternoon, Grandpa and Grandma showed up at Kat's house for a surprise visit.

Dad welcomed them at the door, and while Kat led Grandma away to show her all her latest dog pictures, Grandpa delayed Dad and privately said, "How would you like us to babysit our wonderful granddaughter while you take my lovely daughter on a date?"

"I'd love it; what's the catch."

"I don't know why I ever let someone so suspicious marry my daughter," he lamented.

Dad merely waited,

"Well, actually, I will buy your dinner if, sometime in the course of the evening, you stop by the mall and visit the pet shop."

Dad groaned.

"Wait, there's no obligation. Just watch a demonstration of the puppies, and then you can leave, but you may be surprised."

"I'm only surprised it took this long for Kat to enlist your aid in her puppy scheme, but I can do dinner for free and then tell you and her 'No!' You are just wasting the cost of a dinner."

"Maybe....Maybe not."

Kat's Dad and Mom decided they would get the trip to the pet store over with first so they could go to supper with a clear conscience. Instead, they went to supper, knowing they couldn't say no. The puppies they had seen all met even Dad's high standard of training, and they had to admit Kat was probably ready for the responsibility of a pet of her own. Plus, with the beginning of summer vacation, she would have plenty of time to build habits of responsibility.

The cost of the puppy seemed awfully high, but Grandpa had assured them that was their problem. It didn't keep Dad from feeling bad enough to pay for the dinner himself.

Mom and Dad returned home to find Kat asleep and Grandpa and Grandma waiting expectantly.

"So…?" questioned Grandpa,

Dad just nodded.

Two weeks later, Kat woke up on her birthday and came downstairs to find her Grandparents waiting for her. They wished her Happy Birthday as she ran over to hug them. Approaching the couch, she realized something was moving on a blanket between them.

It was a dog.

Kat scooped the puppy into her arms and hugged it. The little dog calmly let itself be hugged, waiting to be put back down. Kat didn't even notice the tepid response of her new pet. She had a dog. It was her dog. Her dog to love and care for. At that moment, Kat was sure it was the Best Dog in the Whole World.

Grandpa was excited to show off the capable pet. "Watch this," he said to Kat, as one after another, he demonstrated the litany of tricks the little fluffy puppy could do.

It hardly seemed possible, but Kat was even more delighted than before. "Can I try?"

"Sure," said Grandpa, "just take these treats and make sure you give her one as a reward each time she does a trick for you."

Kat quickly used up her first handful of treats, having her puppy beg, dance, roll over, and do all the other tricks she could remember. As she came back to Grandpa for another handful of treats, she had an inspiration, "Do you know what I am going to name her?"

"What?" chorused the family

"Trixie."

That was on Saturday. By Monday evening, Mom and Dad realized they would have to limit how many treats Trixie could get in a day because if it was left up to Kat, she would spend the whole day having her new pet perform its tricks. They found a bowl holding a generous but reasonable amount of food and told Kat that she could only have Trixie do tricks until the food was gone. She could feed it to the puppy while it did tricks or put it in the bowl, but that was the limit.

For two months, every bite of food that Trixie ate came directly from Kat. The young lady seemed never to tire of having her dog do all of its tricks. She had taken the puppy through the neighborhood, showing everyone who would watch her amazing animal. Then, one day, Kat was busy. Not extremely busy, but busy enough that she didn't spend any time with Trixie. When Dad got home from work, he suggested that if the family went with him to do some shopping at the Home Depot, he would take them out to eat afterward. As Kat ran through the kitchen on her way upstairs to her room to get a sweatshirt, she realized that Trixie still hadn't eaten. She figured that the dog would get hungry before they returned home, so she called Trixie and set the bowl down next to her water dish.

"Help yourself, girl. I'll be back," she called, expecting the puppy to start gobbling up the bowl full of treats.

Instead, the dog gave her a puzzled look, turned back to the bowl, looked up again, and whined softly.

"Go ahead, eat it," encouraged Kat as she turned to get her jacket.

When she returned to the kitchen, she saw Trixie sitting in a corner several yards away from her bowl, chewing a bite of her food. When she finished, she rolled over, dashed to her bowl, and snatched another bite. Finishing that, she sat up and begged, then darted over for another bite.

Kat was so puzzled by the dog's actions that she didn't hear her Dad calling until he came back into the house looking for her. Seeing his daughter looking puzzled, he turned to discover the focus of her attention. He was just in time to see Trixie sit up and shake an imaginary hand before she darted over for the next bite. He watched through several more cycles of the dog's strange action, then turned to Kat, "I guess she's not used to getting to eat out of a bowl, Kat, but I'm sure she will soon. Let's get going."

———

Trixie didn't get used to it. Weeks went by, and still, she refused to eat until she had done her tricks. The behavior puzzled the family as time went on. If Trixie wanted to do her tricks before eating, it didn't hurt anybody. But, it remained a mystery.

One morning at breakfast, Grandpa was making his way through the newspaper. He always read the whole thing before he started his day, if not every article, definitely every headline. The second section was devoted to state and local news, and buried on page six was a short article with the headline, "Business owner arrested on 387 counts of animal cruelty." As Grandpa read the story, he made the connection. It described an unusual raid that had been conducted on a large warehouse. Neighbors had complained about the smell from the commercial building. After repeated attempts to contact the owner, law enforcement entered the building and found a dog training arena. The story described the conditions in which the puppies allegedly were kept to facilitate their accelerated training. The unusual smell was apparently from an incinerator used to cremate those puppies who had starved before they could comprehend the training.

The final paragraph listed the retailers where the trained puppies had been marketed, and Grandpa recognized the name of the pet store where they had purchased Trixie. He called the store and realized that they had only recently become aware of the problem. They were worried about liability, but there wasn't much they could do. They offered him a full refund for the puppy or an exchange, but he was pretty sure no one wanted to get rid of Trixie; they just wanted her to stop her ridiculous meal-time ritual.

Grandpa called Dad read him the story and was frankly surprised at how hard the news hit his son-in-law. It had been easy to assume that Dad just didn't like pets, but something more intentional and nuanced seemed to be the case. Grandpa heard him almost thinking out loud,

"So, not only, when we have Trixie do a trick does she relive the terror of their cruelty, but every time she even eats, she lives in fear of not meeting their standard. Poor thing."

When Dad got home that night, he explained to Mom and Kat the reason for Trixie's strange behavior. The first thing they decided was that they wouldn't have Trixie do any more tricks to get a treat. They would only feed her from the bowl.

It didn't work. Trixie still insisted on doing her tricks.

They tried filling her bowl with more than she could possibly eat, trying to convince the young dog that they fed her because they loved her, not because she could do tricks. Maybe it was Dad's imagination, but the new abundance didn't stop the tricks; it was as if Trixie was proud of the overflowing dish. She seemed to interpret it as a reward for her tricks.

Dad contacted a vet whom he knew personally and discussed their unusual pet. The vet was as puzzled as he was.

"If the dog was doing something wrong, I think I know how you could stop it, but if the dog is doing something right for the wrong reason, I'm not sure anyone can change it."

Dad wasn't willing to accept that. He hadn't allowed Kat to even have a dog until he was sure that she would genuinely be able to love and care for it, and now the dog was trapped in a life bounded by the fear of not meeting her standards. Kat loved Trixie, but Trixie couldn't see it. There had to be something He could do.

Dad planned a weekend; he had Kat and Mom stay at Grandma and Grandpa's, and while she was gone, he "forgot" to feed Trixie. He hoped the combination of hunger and joy at seeing Kat return would convince the dog that Kat fed her because of love. There was a chance that Trixie might be upset at him for forgetting her feed, but it would be worth having the dog angry at him if only she would see his child's love.

It did no good. Kat rushed into the house and hugged Trixie, who, as always, let herself be hugged. She filled the bowl with an abundance of her dog food, and they watched as Trixie lay down and played dead for a moment, then darted over and grabbed a mouthful of food.

Kat was old enough to comprehend her father's concern for Trixie, but it was less complicated for her; she just loved Trixie and wanted her to feel loved. She sat in the middle of the floor, watching Trixie go through her ridiculous eating ritual and talking to her pet.

"Don't you see, Trixie, I love you because you are mine. I love your tricks, but they don't make me love you more. I love you because you are mine."

Trixie kept darting past her to grab her mouthful of food, and Dad watched as a tear rolled down Kat's Cheek. There had to be a way to reach their pet.

The next morning, Mom had the most surprising event of their marriage so far. Dad got out of the shower, turned to Mom, who was brushing her hair, and said, "I think we should get another dog."

She stared at him in the mirror and replied, "Who are you? And what did you do with my husband?"

"Just hear me out. If we got a dog, just a plain old mutt that didn't know any tricks or anything, and Trixie saw that we fed and loved him, maybe Trixie would understand that we feed and love her because she is ours, not because she can do tricks."

Mom agreed it was worth a try, so Dad and Kat went out to look for a dog on Saturday. They looked through the paper together and found a want ad.

"Free Puppies."

Dad called the number, and after being sure that they were really free and that they were in no way remarkable, he wrote down the address and took Kat for a ride. When she saw the puppies, she was delighted. They were of no ascertainable breed and had no evidence of any training. The mob of puppies surrounded Kat, and one mottled puppy reached up and began licking Kat's face. She was delighted. She hugged the puppy, and the puppy shivered with delight, and since it didn't have arms to hug her back, it did the next best thing and peed on her.

Her dampened leg didn't dampen her joy; she turned to Dad and said, "Can we keep it?"

Dad nodded.

<hr />

That's how Scruffy became part of the family.

It was months before they got him mostly potty trained, and you never could trust him not to chew on a particularly smelly shoe if it was left in his reach. He definitely was a prime example of a dog who you had to love first and be proud of only much later.

The change in Trixie was noticeable.

She didn't quit doing her tricks; she did them with a new sense of purpose, almost of pride. When they set the bowls of food before each of the dogs, Scruffy would dive in and gobble up all his food. Then, having learned quickly not to touch Trixie's, he would sit and watch her perform one of her tricks, then stalk over for a bite of food. She was clearly aware that she was better than this mutt who could do nothing of value. They could love the newcomer for no reason if they wanted, but she would always know that they loved her because she could do tricks.

So life continued. Kat loved and cared for both dogs, although she had to admit it was easier to love Scruffy because he was so good at loving her back. Dad finally had to accept that there was nothing he could do but wait until the dog chose to believe that they had loved her first.

"We love Him because, He first loved us."

-John

How long has the father had to wait
for you to give up trusting your tricks,
and believe that He loved you first?

The Hungry Soldier

Daniel entered the U.S. Army three days after his high school graduation, which he thought was perfect timing. He had dreamed of being in the Army since he was old enough to understand that his father had made the same choice to serve his country when he was a young man. The first unpleasant realization that struck him concerning army life was not the somewhat overbearing manner of the drill sergeants or even the slightly strenuous nature of the workouts they required. No, for him, the first moment of real panic came when he was told he would have to do his own laundry. For Daniel, this was uncharted territory. In his home, laundry was put in a hamper, and from there, it disappeared and reappeared in his drawers and closet.

For some young people, this might be evidence of parents who feel compelled to raise lazy children. Each year, hundreds or maybe thousands of parents find themselves raising lazy teens, and they don't understand why. They are slightly discomfited by the realization but feel helpless to change the outcome when the reality of their children's laziness fully sinks in. This is because they have forgotten the first weapon in the arsenal of a teen. Teens instinctively know that if they can make it harder to get them to do an "act of work" than it is to actually do the "act of work," most parents will opt to do the "act of work" themselves. This is, in fact, the desired outcome from the teen's viewpoint. Surprisingly, even the peeved comment, "Fine, I'll do it!" doesn't bring on a fit of remorse in the teen. Occasionally, it even inspires the teen to avoid other "acts of work," resulting in teens leaving home without anything but the vaguest idea of how to cook, clean, or do laundry. Fortunately, this lack of knowledge is often offset by an uncanny ability to kill virtual zombies, matched with a stunning speed sending text messages.

For Daniel, however, none of this was the case. His ignorance of domestic chores came from the fact that he had made himself quite valuable in other endeavors. His father had left the service and begun a contracting business. This meant that as soon as Daniel was old enough to help, there was plenty of work for him with his father. By the time he was twelve, he was a capable carpenter and loved to spend his free time working with his father. By age 14, he had discovered a second outlet for his craftsmanship. He began building boats. His kayaks were remarkable, and he began taking custom orders. His days were full of school, his afternoons occupied with building, and his evenings were spent in his father's shop crafting beautiful boats. His mother and father were content to see him invest his time in hard work as long as he kept up with his school work (which he typically did during the long bus ride to school.) The fact that he didn't know the first thing about laundry or cooking wasn't a concern.

So Daniel, a.k.a. Private Brown, had to figure out the mysterious workings of a washing machine at basic training. By watching others and asking a few questions, he got the hang of it. Although, it must be said that the Army knew what it was doing when it issued underwear the color of dirty water. There is nothing in the drab clothing of a soldier by which you can accurately measure whether it is clean or dirty. What matters to a private is whether the clothes stink, not some commercially inspired concept of "bold, bright colors" or "downy soft texture."

Daniel proceeded through Basic training with no other significant surprises but with one overriding impression. He was always hungry. His young, growing body had a rate of metabolism that made short work of even the calorie-rich MREs, which were sometimes issued for meals. Visits to the chow hall offered a bit more food, but seldom with sufficient time to eat all you wanted. To Daniel's delight, his Advance Individual Training offered more time to enjoy the chow hall, as well as the freedom to go to the shopette to get some snacks in the evening. But the new freedom also allowed him to go to the gym. He found an increasing joy in the strength of his body and spent many hours pushing himself to peak physical performance. His metabolism was a roaring oven, consuming calories as fast as he could shovel them in, which he did every chance he got. But still, there was a constant hunger, especially in the late evening when the chow hall was closed, and his appetite was returning after a long session in the weight room, in the pool, or on the track.

When Daniel arrived at his first duty station, things continued much the same. His room in the barracks included a small refrigerator with a tiny freezer section, allowing him to include ice cream with the other snacks he used to fight the evening onset of hunger. But he found that after a month or so, he was snacked out. He wanted real food for his very real hunger.

One of the highlights in his life was when his squad leader, Sergeant Mason, would invite him over to his home. Sgt. Brent Mason was "older," which is a matter of skewed perspective for new soldiers. (In Daniel's basic training platoon, a private who was 31 got the nickname Gramps.) But Sgt. Mason was married and had three sons. He and his wife Sarah felt sorry for the soldiers who had to live in the barracks and ensured they got regular invitations to come and eat real home-cooked food. Mrs. Mason, who always looked around for her mother when the soldiers called her that, had grown up with six brothers, so she understood the amount of food that a teenager could consume and knew how to hold her own in a world of young men. She loved cooking for the soldiers in her husband's unit. The more a person ate, the more often she would invite that person over, so it was probably inevitable that Daniel would become a regular at their home. Most Friday nights, he would have supper with their family, and often, he could return the favor by watching the boys while Sgt. Mason and his wife attended a movie or took a walk.

For Daniel, that took care of one night a week, but it only made him miss good food more on the other nights. His barracks had a day room where soldiers could play pool or watch TV. One corner was devoted to a kitchen, including a refrigerator, stove, microwave, and an odd assortment of pans and utensils left behind by earlier generations of soldiers. Daniel noticed that some soldiers would make themselves a snack in the evening, ramen being a favorite. It looked good, but he had no idea how to make it, and he felt reluctant to ask anyone and display his ignorance. The dream of cooking something to eat in the evening grew, so he resolved to ask Mrs. Mason if he ever got the chance.

On his next visit to the Mason's, he was waiting for that opportunity. It finally came when Sgt. Mason went to take one of the boys a glass of water. They paused the movie they were watching, and while they waited, Daniel gathered the courage to bring up the topic.

"Mrs. Mason, do you mind if I ask you a question?" queried Daniel.

Sarah perked up a bit. Usually, when one of the male soldiers sought out her female perspective privately, it was about meeting a girl. "Not at all," she answered.

"Is it hard to make ramen noodles?"

"What do you mean?"

"You know, those packages you can buy with the curly noodles. A lot of guys get them to eat. I just wondered if they are hard to make."

"No, not at all. You just drop them in boiling water for 2 to 3 minutes until they are soft. Add the flavoring, and they're ready to eat."

"Can I ask you one more question?"

"Sure."

"Where do you get boiling water?"

Sarah stopped herself from laughing when she saw the serious look on Daniel's face. He really didn't know. It was hard to think about needing to learn something so simple, but if he needed to know, she was willing to teach him.

"Say, would you like me to teach you? I think we have a package of Ramen noodles."

With the kids finally asleep, Sgt. Mason came downstairs and found Sarah and Daniel in the kitchen, watching a pot of water on the stove. "Is watching water boil really more interesting than the movie?" quipped Brent

Sarah briefly explained that Daniel was interested in learning to cook, so she was showing him how to make ramen noodles. After a bowl of ramen and the remainder of the movie, Daniel left for the barracks with a new passion: He wanted to learn more about cooking. Back at the Mason's, Sarah headed to bed, chuckling. "And to think," she mumbled, "I thought it was about a girl."

Several weeks later, on one of Daniel's now regular trips to the commissary for another week's worth of ramen, he noticed the picture on the package. It showed the ramen noodles as a base for a delicious-looking combination of meat strips, pea pods, bamboo shoots, cashews, and bean sprouts. He checked the other flavored packages and saw similar concoctions with shrimp and chicken. His first thought was to ask Sarah about it the next time he visited, but something prompted him to try it himself. Using the picture on the package as a shopping list, he wandered the aisles of the commissary, looking for the various items. That night began the first of many experiments on making what became known in the barracks as "Killer Ramen." Daniel quickly became the master of ramen soup. He always had an exciting collection of vegetables, meat, and sauces in the box he kept in the shared refrigerator. It became almost a barracks SOP (Standard Operating Procedure) to drop what you were doing and head for the day room about 15 minutes after you saw Daniel walking that way. If you were lucky and close to the front of the line, you might get his "leftovers," which were usually plentiful. Daniel was learning to love feeding hungry soldiers as much as he loved learning to cook.

Both interests expanded. Daniel gained confidence as a cook, and by the time he bought his first cookbook, he realized that it wasn't especially helpful. He preferred to imagine the flavors he was hungry for then try to create the dish he had imagined. He did find one useful book, but it was less of a cookbook than a reference book that helped him understand the properties of the various ingredients. Admittedly, he had many failed experiments, some so bad they got fed directly to the garbage, but most were edible, and many were excellent. Most nights, at a little after eleven, the residents of the barracks would head down to the day room, on which someone had posted a sign drawn on an MRE box that declared, "Daniel's Kitchen; If you leave hungry, it's your own fault." Daniel welcomed everyone to divide up what he had made among themselves. Sometimes, it was little more than a few bites each, but usually, Daniel made sure there was sufficient for the expected number of hungry guests. To help with the cost, an unobtrusive cocoa box with a hole in the lid marked "groceries" stood on the counter. It helped a bit, but the bulk of the cost came from Daniel's pocket.

Daniel always made a special meal on the first night back from the field. When his own platoon was out, it was held the night after they returned, but when one of the other platoons spent time in the field, he made sure they were welcomed home with an abundant meal. This was so good that soldiers who lived off-post occasionally asked him if they could invite their wives for the event.

Only a few bothered to consider that these meals could cost Daniel quite a bit of money, and Sgt. Mason was the only one who ever asked him about it. Concerned that Daniel was being taken advantage of, he spoke to him privately one day. "Hey, Brown, how much did that meal cost last night?"

"I don't know, sergeant; I had a lot of the stuff already," he evaded.

"How much?" Brent insisted.

"About $150, I think."

"That's a lot; you sure you can afford it?"

"I'm good."

"Why?" Sgt. Mason asked.

"Why what?"

"Why everything? Why do you cook so much? Why won't you charge people? What do you get out of it anyway?"

"You should ask Sarah," answered Daniel.

"How is she connected?"

"She taught me. Or at least she pointed me in the direction to discover it, but I'm sure she knows it."

"Knows what?"

The impatience in Sgt. Mason's voice told him he would need to answer clearly. "Knows what it's like to feed people when they are hungry. Most people eat just because it's that time of day. But there are a few times when people are hungry, and feeding them then is the most satisfying thing a person can do. Late at night, after a week in the field, or after months in the barracks, as Sarah does. That's when they are hungry, and feeding them then is worth whatever it costs."

"Funny hobby, Brown."

"It's a funny world, sergeant."

Six years and one re-enlistment later, Daniel was ready to leave the Army. He had saved up enough money to start his own restaurant. Many hours of careful thought had gone into the plan, and he had spent his last year of enlistment getting many of the pieces into place. The outer suburbs of many moderate-sized cities have traded their family-owned restaurants for franchises along their main highways, creating a glut of shuttered eateries in the dying business district. He found such a place in the proper price range for his budget. He knew that the location would make it difficult to compete head to head with high-volume franchises, who could afford both to trim prices and advertise extensively, heavy hitters when matched up against his idealistic passion. But, one can never predict the appeal of quirkiness, and Daniel's restaurant was a hit, not just because of Daniel's carefully thought-out business plan, but also due to his guileless demeanor.

Daniel figured that it was *his* restaurant, which he was, to begin with, subsidizing with *his own* money, so he ought to be able to run it the way *he* liked. In terms of food, it meant that there was no such thing as the regular menu. Each day, he published two delicious specials for lunch and another option was added for dinner. Within each choice, there were various ways in which the meal could be customized. Because of this, Daniel took all of the orders himself. He always had assistants working who could be trusted to prepare each basic meal, but, as with the placing of the order, the final minutes of each meal were left in Daniel's hands.

Over the years of dreaming and planning, Daniel had tried out hundreds of names for his restaurant. His final choice was taken from a comment Sarah made one night when the whole squad was over to Sgt. Mason's for a fish fry. Brett had planned a fishing trip for the day, and the fish had been dumb and hungry. After cleaning and breading the fillets, Sarah realized there was more food than the house full of fishermen could eat. That was when she suggested that the house needed a big neon sign on the roof saying "Hungry Soldiers here," which she could turn on whenever there were leftovers.

The mental picture stayed with Daniel for a long time, and in his search for a name, the vision returned. For a while, he considered putting on some airs and using the French translation "*Un soldat enfamme*" as the title, but in the long run, the simplicity of The Hungry Soldier won out. It was a title, an autobiography, and a mission statement all in one.

Ordering at The Hungry Soldier was more like a conversation. After the patron made their initial selection, Daniel conducted a little interview based on which he would make notes helping him customize the meal, the garnish, or the presentation with what most considered an almost uncanny prescience. Even when he missed his guess, people were touched by his personal commitment to each meal. But that wasn't the real secret. Before the patrons were even allowed to hear the specials for the day, Daniel would interrogate them on the level of their hunger. Most often, guests were greeted as they came in with what, to Daniel, seemed like the most important question. "Are you hungry?" New guests were taken aback by the question. It wasn't the *pro forma* "Table or a booth?" or "Can I get you something to drink?" It was blunt and somewhat refreshing. Hunger was what eating was supposed to be all about. And Daniel, in his naive manner, wouldn't let you avoid the question. He never let one person answer for the group. He queried each individual.

He was practical enough that he didn't actually turn customers away. Still, it wasn't unheard of for him to put customers off. When someone's answer about their hunger was non-committal, Daniel was known to suggest, rather forcefully, that they take a walk while he cooked their meal so that by the time he was done, they would have achieved a proper intensity of appetite. The suggestion wasn't just a joke. There was a pleasant park within a block of the restaurant, and Daniel's enthusiastic description of the path around the small lake within the park convinced many to take him up on his suggestion.

Successful restaurants almost always have a gimmick or a niche, something to set them apart or something you can't get anywhere else. Those unique qualities are the most effective advertising available. They bring people back, and they keep people talking. The Hungry Soldier did just that; as a matter of fact, Daniel's effect reached beyond just the restaurant. Many customers found that since Daniel's interrogation, they couldn't escape the link between eating and hunger, finding themselves amazed at how often that link was ignored.

Whatever all the reasons were, The Hungry Soldier grew. It became enormously popular, progressing from full tables to reserved tables to waiting lists to a bigger building, which quickly filled to capacity. Daniel's cooking began attracting attention not just from the customer base but also from critical publications. The presence of food critics became more and more common, but if anything, Daniel was harder on them. He asserted that no one had the right to judge food if they ate it when they weren't hungry. If their assessment didn't measure how well the food fed them, then they were not judging food by its purpose, which Daniel likened to judging a dog show by how well the dogs could fly.

Some food critics found his badgering charming compared with the sycophantic behavior that usually followed the discovery of their critical connections. One to whom a nice walk in the park was suggested initially balked at the idea. But while he was making excuses, one of Daniel's regular customers rolled up to him in a wheelchair. The critic never could decide whether the whole incident was staged and, if so, how, but Daniel volunteered to have him push a lovely elderly lady in a wheelchair around the park. He could hardly refuse the assignment without looking and feeling like a jerk, and he came back from the walk hungry and delighted and met by the best meal he had ever tasted, which to Daniel was no coincidence.

In fact, this man, Mark, a writer for the food section of the nearest major newspaper, became one of Daniel's closest personal friends. And it was Mark who relentlessly pestered Daniel about the need to grow.

"Danny boy, when people have to make their reservations too far in advance, they lose interest. You want to be busy enough to let people know you're popular but not so busy they go elsewhere." Mark opined, "It's touchy business wooing the customers."

"I don't want to woo them; I want to feed them," Daniel countered. "Besides, I couldn't run a second restaurant," he said, knowing that this was the point at which Mark would eventually arrive.

"You wouldn't have to run the restaurant; you would have other people run it."

"But it wouldn't be as good if I couldn't be there to do the cooking and meet the customers."

"It wouldn't have to be, given your reputation. The name would be enough to draw the customers. Branding and marketing attract people more than quality."

"Silly me! I thought it was hunger that made people want to eat."

"There you go again," said Mark, feigning exasperation, "yammering about the hunger thing. Someday, you will have to realize you aren't cooking for the soldiers in the barracks anymore. You're cooking for slightly overweight, grossly overfed, fashionably bored people with too much money and a need to find the newest trend to prove their hipness. That's the segment of society that makes you a profit or leaves you high and dry."

"Oh, you're a critic and a cynic, too!" laughed Daniel. "If my opinion of my customers was as low as your opinion of your readers, even I wouldn't want to eat here. How about I keep cooking for hungry people, and you keep telling them where to get good food, and we'll see how things come out."

"Ok, ok," conceded Mark, "but remember now that we're friends, I can't go propping up your business in my paper. Journalistic integrity and whatnot."

"The only thing you ever propped up was your feet in front of the TV. Now get out of my kitchen. I have work to do."

"All right, I'm outta here, but I'm not giving up. See you around." Mark left thinking about ways to convince his friend to grow his business. He was a gifted cook and a remarkable, if a bit eccentric, marketer. But he had so much to learn about business. His idealism was charming, but somehow, it needed to be packaged so that more people could encounter it. Mark valued, perhaps more than he would admit, the focus on hunger. The first night at The Hungry Soldier had really shaken him out of a life that was becoming increasingly complacent. But if more people were to have such an experience, Daniel would have to take growth seriously.

Mark envisioned a whole series of restaurants that would follow the principle of Daniel's premise. He knew that the key would be for Daniel to teach a philosophy course disguised as a cooking class. Mark became excited as the brainstorm continued. He would ask Daniel to teach a small group of cooks, including himself, the hungry soldier cooking method. From the students, Daniel would be able to develop talented assistants to run the new restaurants. Even though Mark couldn't openly tout The Hungry Soldier, given his personal connection, he could write a unique series of articles during his time in the class.

Mark almost turned the car around to tell Daniel his great idea. But he knew Daniel would resist anything that distracted him from feeding his "Hungry" customers. But there might be another way.

Over the next few weeks, Mark began encouraging many of the young chefs and prospective restaurateurs he met in the course of his work to ask Daniel to mentor them. All of them responded enthusiastically to the idea, and with Mark's support, they got the courage to begin pestering Daniel with the suggestion. He was pleasantly surprised and somewhat flattered by the sudden interest in his cooking, especially by people he knew had far more formal education on the subject than he did. Not suspecting that Mark was the cause of it, Daniel shared his dilemma with his friend. He reported on the interest being expressed by a wide variety of prospective students.

Daniel was encouraged by Mark's excitement about the project. Mark even suggested that he would enroll, if such a class were ever conducted. But Daniel was still beset by doubts. "I don't know the first thing about teaching. And I don't even know that much about cooking. The only thing I am an expert on is being hungry," admitted Daniel.

"Nonsense!" countered Mark. "You don't need to know how to teach. You know how you learned. Just help people take the steps you took."

Daniel looked thoughtful for a moment, then responded tentatively, "I could do that."

The class was to be held at the original restaurant, which had been closed when the Hungry Soldier was moved to the new site. Now, it was used as a makeshift office where Daniel had space to pile up the fruits of his procrastination in the realm of bookkeeping. The various papers and correspondence were moved to one corner of the dining room, the kitchen equipment was dusted off, and the pantry and freezers were filled with an extensive variety of supplies ready for Daniel's first class of fourteen students. The classes began at six o'clock in the morning so that the instruction would be finished in time for many of the students to work the supper rush at their respective restaurants. Daniel, too, was unwilling to leave The Hungry Soldier alone for a whole day. This allowed him to work half the day there after he finished teaching his class at three o'clock. He also had another reason for starting early: he wanted to get his students up too early to eat breakfast.

As expected, most of the students showed up yawning through their first cup of coffee, hoping to leisurely ease into the morning. They took their seats at the chairs arranged around a prep table, which had been moved into the dining area, and waited for their first lecture. Promptly at six, Daniel strode in and spent the first fifteen seconds taking roll from a list he had apparently memorized. The next ten seconds he spent explaining that a van was parked outside and they were to proceed to it. Daniel led the way, almost running to the vehicle.

As he explained, once they were all buckled in and on their way, good ingredients were the first component of good cooking. He was taking them to his food suppliers for a tour. The drive took forty-five minutes, during which Daniel peppered them with "getting to know you" type questions. Well, the first few were; then the focus quickly changed. Soon, Daniel was probing to find answers to what, to him, seemed like the most important question. "When were you the hungriest you have ever been?" Under his interrogation, some interesting stories came out. One was about a camping trip experienced as a child when bears had eaten the groceries, leaving little for the family. Another told of running out of money in college and having nothing but a jar of peanut butter to last a week.

What surprised Daniel was not the number of hungry stories but the lack of them. Several students could not seriously remember a time in their lives when they had been hungry. Through his interrogation, he realized that some had never even allowed themselves the hunger of anticipation. For some, even the delight of such famous meals as a grandmother's Thanksgiving dinner had always been dulled by snacking rather than sharpened by an hour or two of fasting. Daniel thought that this field trip might really be helpful.

When he arrived at the warehouse, he parked on the far side of the parking lot. Pleading that he didn't want to risk having the borrowed van side-swiped by one of the semis picking up and delivering food, he led them quite a distance across the parking lot and in the back door of the warehouse. The operation was impressive. Palletized food was being loaded and unloaded with an anthill-like scurry of forklifts and pallet jacks. Daniel, who seemed to know his way around, shepherded his group through the aisles and in and out of departments, stopping to show them different products he used and explaining various processes to preserve freshness and assure quality. It might not have been a very interesting tour, but at least Daniel didn't belabor any of the points. It wasn't like he indulged in mind-numbing, canned speeches like you might expect on such a tour. It was more like a five-year-old showing you his grandpa's farm. He was constantly running off in different directions, saying, "Hey, come here, you gotta see this." His excitement was infectious but also a little irritating. He scampered back and forth, covering the whole warehouse and all of its departments in the most inefficient manner. By late forenoon, the class was getting a bit worn out from the tour and was looking forward to the fruition of one of the rumors started by a class member. He had suggested that they were bound to be brought up to the front offices and offered a smorgasbord of samples. "That's what they always do," he asserted.

And indeed, they would have had Daniel not refused. Shortly after noon, the class made the sojourn to the van, and Daniel drove back to the classroom, using the whole trip to describe some of his favorite meals with a vividness that made more than one mouth water. Back at the old restaurant, the class filed into their seats as Daniel wheeled a cart full of an astonishing array of ingredients out to the prep table. The class waited expectantly to be taught by the master, although it might be said that some of the class were more eager to get to taste the outcome at this point.

Just as Daniel drew a breath, preparing to begin the instruction, his phone rang. Quickly, he checked the caller ID. He looked apologetically at the class and offered, "I really have to take this."

The class watched and listened as he answered the call and was startled by Daniel's outburst: "What!! That can't be right. I know I took care of that." There was a pause. "We can't file that today; I'm busy." The conversation continued for a moment, ending with Daniel's discouraged concession: "Oh, all right, I'll do it."

Hanging up the phone, he looked at the gathered faces. "I am very sorry," he apologized. "Something has come up. I'll try to take care of it quickly." Then, looking at the disappointed faces, he asked, "Say, are you guys hungry?" On that point, there was unanimous consensus. "Look, you go ahead and use what's here to make something for your lunch. I'll be back as soon as I can." And with that, Daniel was gone.

They watched him drive off toward the new restaurant, then looked around at each other. No one knew what to do precisely. Most might have just waited for him to return, but no one wanted to skip lunch after the field trip that had become more like a forced march. Although they all worked daily preparing food, it was unusual to be given no direction beyond their hunger. One by one, the students began poking around the table for something to eat. There was a nice variety, and the ingredients looked delicious. So slowly, people began to get inspirations. Some opted for the convenience of a sandwich, but with all the different ingredients, they couldn't help but add a bit of this and a bit of that. Others saw something that reminded them of a dish they knew they wanted to prepare. One who realized that elbow room would be in short supply called out, "I'll set the table and do dishes if you all make a bit extra for me."

The next hour appeared to have more in common with a food fight than a culinary education experience. But, as the class worked to make themselves lunch, an almost party-like atmosphere developed, and by the time everyone brought their dishes to the table everyone was excited to taste what the others had made. There was nothing formal, just a "Hey, can I try that?" and a "Who wants to trade me something for this half a sandwich?" As the meal was winding down, Daniel returned. Looking at the table, he pulled up a chair and apologized profusely. But as he took in the array of food around him, he said, "Hey, I'm hungry! Does anybody have anything left?" Some of the students tentatively offered their teacher a bit of leftover this or the last few bites of that.

Usually, it isn't a good idea to have the person talking also be the person eating, but no one minded the fact that Daniel, between bites of food and compliments, started telling stories about the Army. They were all somewhat food-related, and they were all hilarious. When Daniel had finished all the food that was left and his story about when their platoon traded twenty cases of MREs and the battalion commander's office chair for a camel which they barbecued, he looked up and said, "Ok, it's three, but I suppose we need to clean up a bit before we end."

Sheepishly, the volunteer raised his hand and said, "I guess that's my job. "See, we sort of made a deal…"

"Great!" Daniel smiled, "You wash, I'll dry, and we'll see the rest of you tomorrow morning."

———————

By Thursday, Mark knew he had to say something to save Daniel's cooking school. Things couldn't go on like they were. True, it had been a fun four days, but there still had been no formal teaching. Monday, it was the warehouse; Tuesday, a butcher shop, a farm, and a dairy; Wednesday, they started at three to spend the morning running to and fro in a bakery, and today was no better. They had gone and walked miles in the fields of a half dozen farmers, as if seeing the carrot in its natural environment was going to teach anyone to be a chef.

Mark knew that the other students were getting into the swing of the schedule. They almost expected the daily interruption, which inevitably seemed to come as they were about to begin the daily lecture: the daily "near miss," as it was being called. But Mark, as the most mature member of the class, also realized that when the students realized they had wasted the two-week course with nothing to show for their effort, there was bound to be a backlash. He tried to diminish how peeved he felt personally that his idea of using the course as material for a series of articles was not working out. If he tried to describe the week's activities, he was afraid Daniel would move beyond quirky to crazy.

But the problem was Daniel wouldn't care. It was like he had stepped back in time and was leading his squad in the Army. He was more concerned about his new buddies than about any implication for his restaurant career. Mark realized it was time to help him get on track. He had to stop him from being led astray by the enthusiasm with which the rest of the class embraced his lack of plans for each day.

That night, Mark stopped by the Hungry Soldier shortly before closing time, and, as expected, Daniel was hard at work. He met Mark at the door with the standard question, "Are you hungry?"

"Why do you think I waited till almost ten? I didn't want to get sent on a wild goose chase."

"What are you hungry for?"

"Surprise me." That was Daniel's favorite order and, coming this late in the evening, it almost ensured that Mark would get a chance to talk with Daniel when he came out to talk about the food.

Mark was finishing his supper when Daniel came out with a mug of tea and sat down across the table from him. Mark could see that Daniel was exhausted, and he almost avoided the subject of school. But Daniel needed the help. It would all be for nothing if he didn't keep the school on track.

After a question about the supper, which was truly remarkable, Daniel asked, "So, are you enjoying the class?" A twinkle in his eye let Mark know that Daniel had him figured out. He knew Mark had an issue to raise. He was letting Mark know, "Go ahead, let me have it."

"Look, Daniel, I know you are having a lot of fun, and I know that the students are enjoying it, but you are making a serious mistake the way you are leading the class."

"I told you I didn't know how to teach," Daniel commented with a smile.

"I'm serious. There needs to be a lesson plan—a list of topics that the students know they are learning—something tangible that you can take credit for teaching. Otherwise, the school will never grow."

"I never wanted to grow the school."

"But you need the school," continued Mark, "The only way you are going to be able to expand and open more restaurants is by training people to cook like you do. You have to teach them your methods and procedures so that they can do what you do. It's the only way you can grow. You know you won't be able to keep doing what you are doing forever. And what happens to the Hungry Soldier then?"

"I suppose it closes."

"And you're OK with that."

"When I can't keep doing this anymore, why would I care?" When no answer was forthcoming, Daniel continued. "About ten years ago, I discovered something. In a funny world full of chaos and deception, only one thing doesn't lie. Your hunger. You can try to fill it with substitutes, but the hunger stays until it gets fed. You can try to ignore it, but the hunger always returns. But I also discovered that I like feeding hungry people. No, I love feeding hungry people. If I can use my restaurant to do that, I am happy. Tired, but happy. I have no desire to own a restaurant for any other reason.

"When you put me up to this school idea, and don't pretend you didn't, I only did what you told me to do. You said, and I quote, 'You don't need to know how to teach. You know how you learned. Just help people take the steps you took.' I thought maybe it was worth doing. And now I am sure. I'm not trying to start a franchise or make my restaurant immortal; I'm not even trying to teach anyone to cook. I am trying to teach fourteen people about hunger. And I suspect only thirteen have been learning that lesson. But maybe number fourteen wants to start."

Mark smiled. "Maybe he does."

"Blessed are those who hunger and thirst for
righteousness, for they shall be filled."

-Jesus

We have videos and study books,
commentaries and Bible dictionaries,
radio preachers and christian colleges.
And don't forget all the video clips on social media.
God has been carefully packaged
to attract our interest
and increase His marketability.
Maybe what we need is hunger.

The Extra Sixteenth

Guiding, especially for fishermen, is an interesting profession. Obviously, the people who take on such a career must be committed anglers, and the vast majority of them are, but how successful a fisherman do you want your guide to be? You want him to be able to catch fish; after all, who would hire a guide who couldn't? But do you want your guide to catch more fish than you do? Some people would answer that question, "Of course. The guide is the expert. Who would trust someone worse than yourself?"

The opposing point of view holds that having paid good money, the client wants to feel like a mighty fisherman, so the guide should carefully avoid showing the client up. That may be the opposing point of view, but it may be hard to actually find someone who holds it. Sure, most guides observe the convention of waiting to be invited to fish, but once they are fishing, it's pretty hard not to want to do everything you can to come out on top. These people were fishermen long before they were guides. If the competitive spirit hadn't run deep, the guide probably wouldn't have become the kind of fisherman valued as a guide. So basically, no matter how professional he is, if you invite your guide to fish, your guide probably wants to catch the biggest fish of the day.

Now, such human foibles can be smiled at, especially in the face of the reality of fishing, where lady luck always plays the trump card. Fishing legends are sprinkled with tales of trophy fish taken on a snoopy pole and a piece of bubble gum while the expert angler flails the water uselessly with his thousands of dollars of gear. Most guides can accept that, some with grace and genuine joy at their client's impressive catch, others with a façade of professionalism, as if helping someone haul in a fish that dwarfs their best efforts is just (ho-hum) an everyday thing. Some even indulge in a bit of grumpiness, but few actually do something about it. Ray was the exception.

Ray had worked as an electrician for fourteen years before he had scraped together enough money to launch his guiding service, and the electrician's license helped him provide for his family through the winters. But the guiding service, now in its seventh year, was beginning to show enough profit to carry him through the slower winter fishing season without having to wear his nose down on the proverbial grindstone. Ray's portfolio included a number of impressive fish. The wall of the office from which he ran the guiding service was plastered with a series of rather monotonous shots when taken as a whole. When examined individually, they were quite impressive. There were many photos of satisfied customers holding up their prize fish, but if you were observant, you would notice that there was always a picture of Ray next to it holding up a bigger fish. Ray worked hard to always have the biggest fish.

It would be hard to deny that this drive benefited his clients. He knew where to find big fish and how to get them into the boat.

His specialty was big northern pike. Early in his fishing career, he realized that jumbo northern were under-fished in northern Minnesota. The glamour of the walleyes and the brute strength of the muskellunge eclipsed the reputation of the northern pike. This meant that almost every good-sized lake had a significant population of large specimens, which were rarely pursued. Ray had discovered that a casual angler seldom used anything that would tempt one of these monsters, and those pursuing a trophy would inevitably be seduced to try their luck at one of the over-fished musky lakes. Ray also found that when pulling in a twenty-plus pound fish, his clients suddenly lost any snobbishness they might have harbored towards the lowly northern. Ray's life-long hope was to set a new state record for the biggest northern. Undoubtedly, it would help his business, but the desire was much more personal.

His cherished ambition was given a breath of hope when catch-and-release fishing came into vogue. The Minnesota Department of Natural Resources created a new category of records: catch and release. Trophy fish returned to the lake could still compete for a record if captured on film, witnessed, and measured. A measurement of the girth and length could be used to compute a total weight, which could compete for its own spot in the record annals. Ray dreamed about seeing his name there and figured that as one of the most consistent big northern fishermen, he had a good chance of someday succeeding. His biggest fear was that someday, the record fish would get on his client's line, and he would be cheated out of the goal he had spent so much time pursuing.

Initially, that thought just hung out in the back of his mind. But, with the growth of his guiding service and the regularity with which he fished in the company of others, the thought developed into a fear, a fear which grew and grew so that whenever a client had a big fish on, Ray would be on pins and needles until he finally measured the fish and saw that it had missed the record. One day, as he was breathing a sigh of relief at a fish that had missed the record by just a few inches, an idea came to him.

———◦◦◦———

Measuring a trophy fish always presents a problem. Anyone who has landed a big northern or musky knows that the real fight begins when the fish gets in the boat. A fish that has been fought to exhaustion will suddenly find a new burst of energy when it is set into the boat. At that point, its natural instincts take over, and it will thrash with an innate knowledge that it must find a way back to the water or die. The easiest solution is to measure the fish while it is still in the water along the boat. Spent from the struggle, it often will float quietly alongside the boat, making it easy to measure. Ray had a special "yardstick" he used, although since many of the fish he caught surpassed the 36" mark, it was a 60" yardstick. He had purchased it from a sporting goods store. It carried the impressive name "Monster Measure" and was made of buoyant material that would float alongside the fish. One end had a cross piece to be held against the fish's nose. In the middle, it had a length of flexible measuring tape to tighten around the fish's body. The whole thing was printed in oversized numbers on a hi-vis orange background so that the relevant measurements of the fish were easily readable in a photo.

Ray realized that he could easily prevent the disaster of having a client, who was just out for a day of fishing, grab the glory for which he had worked so hard by having a second measuring stick with just a little added to each inch. A sixteenth added to each inch would be almost indistinguishable, but over the length of a possible record fish, it could cut nearly three inches off the measurement, ensuring that a client didn't just ease over the mark and steal "his" record. He set to work making just such a measuring stick. When he was finished, it looked identical to the production model, except that it had a fluorescent green background instead of orange, and, of course, it was longer than the accurate ruler. Ray painstakingly copied every detail, including the logo, so that in the picture, there would be nothing to suggest it was in any way different.

He made a special rack under the steering console of his fishing boat where he could hang both yardsticks. The green one was just a little higher up and harder to reach, but it was always there in the event that it was needed. And in the year since he had made it, there had only been one occasion when he had pulled it out. As his client was landing a nice fish, Ray had been scared enough to pull out the green stick just to make sure. The fish wouldn't have been a record (it probably had enough length, but it was unusually skinny) so Ray told himself the ruse didn't really bother his conscience.

In that instance, his client was a businessman from Iowa who went fishing once a year with Ray. It wasn't like he was a committed fisherman, and he still had a great fish to brag about and a beautiful picture to hang on his wall. The chances that someone would know that the "Monster Measure" had never been produced in green were pretty slim. If he had been the one to catch the fish, he would rather have missed the record by a few inches than to have been edged out by less than an inch on the girth. At least that is what he told himself... again and again.

The fact that he had to keep explaining it away to himself was probably a hint from his conscience, but every time he considered getting rid of the green stick, he thought with horror about how he would have felt that day if his coveted record had gone to a car dealer from Iowa who had grown up thinking bullheads were a sport fish. The bright green "Monster Measure" stayed in the boat.

Ray will always remember August 5th. Partly because it is his son's birthday, but it's not the memory of that event he carries as a burden multiplied by the fact he can tell no one about it.

He had met the day's anglers early at the boat ramp on one of his favorite lakes. They were a lovely couple who had fished with him twice before. Neither was a particularly avid angler, but their son was. He was so avid, perhaps rabid was a better word, that he lacked the patience to fish with his Dad. He was a wealthy stock trader who tried to fish with the same intensity as he traded in the pit, so he would hire Ray to take his parents out, knowing that when they gathered in the evening, they would be able to enjoy each other's company a lot more reminiscing about a day of fishing, than if they had experienced it together, a mistake which he had made several times in the past.

Clint and Anita were delightful clients. They were always satisfied with their catch, sincerely enjoying the beauty of the lake. Once they had caught a few pounds of small fish, enough to take home for a fish fry, they enjoyed rigging up for trophy northern pike. They would never dream of acting uppity, so they always invited Ray to fish with them, which was why he was willing to take them to one of his favorite lakes. It amounted to getting paid to do what he loved most—stalking the state record northern.

Ray found a sand bar where some 1-2 pound walleyes were feeding. Three-quarters of an hour later, Clint and Anita had their limit of eaters, and it was still early enough to try for a lunker northern while they were transitioning to the deeper waters to deal with the heat of the day.

Ray had learned how to anticipate this move. It was what made the difference between musky fishing and northern. The northern pike differs only slightly from the muskellunge, but one of those differences is their optimum oxygen level. In hot weather, the northern will move to the cooler water, where their oxygen consumption goes down during the day, returning to the shallows in the evening when they can feed in the shallows. Ray had discovered that the journey to deep water follows a predictable path--if you're good at predicting and a bit lucky. Twice before that season, he had caught multiple "big" northern along a drop-off leading out of a bay. The multiple hits made him think this was a regular path, and he hoped today wouldn't disappoint him. The bay was on the southeast side of the lake, so it had been shaded longer, and now, as the sun finally crested the ridge overlooking the lake, the bay was bathed in sun, and the big northern might be following their route out to the deep water.

Or there might be nothing, but that's the charm of fishing.

Rigged for big northern, with a flashy harness holding a live bait fish that could have held its own with the walleyes in the live box, Ray's boat crawled along the mouth of the bay. A slight breeze wafted across the lake and Anita set her rod in a holder so that she could get some coffee and treats out of the cooler she always brought along. Ray usually disdained people who brought fancy lunches along when they fished, but previous years' experience had proved to him that Anita's snacks were much preferable to washing down a bite of jerky with a swig of coke.

She pulled out a Tupperware container filled with a twisted, baked piece of dough drizzled with a braised butter glaze. Ray's mouth began to water as she poured him a cup of rich coffee. She passed a cup of the steaming, fragrant brew to her husband and was about to hand Ray the baked goods when there was a rattle from her rod holder.

The initial onslaught of even a relatively small northern can make you think you have a monster, but when the screaming of the drag on Anita's reel did not slow down, Ray's attention was drawn away from the goodies and back to the fishing. He started making a slow arc to the left to allow her maximum space to play the fish, continuing moving forward at trolling speed to keep the line taught. Within thirty seconds of the strike, Ray began to suspect it was a big fish, and by the time he and Clint had reeled in their lines, he guessed it was a trophy.

Four minutes passed before they caught their first glimpse of the fish, and with that first glimpse, Ray figured he would need the green stick. He had it out and ready by the time Anita, refusing help from either Clint or Ray, had the massive pike alongside the boat. And now, after a vigorous fight, the big fish was content to lie alongside the boat, hardly moving. Clint had the camera out and was taking pictures. But before Anita attempted to lift it up, they snapped a picture to verify its size. The green monster measure floated alongside the fish and was snugged tight by the measuring tape around the girth. A picture with Anita and Ray showing the relevant measurements would have been sufficient to register the pike as a record, but even before the measurement was finalized, Ray knew that he had been premature in using the green stick. It was a nice fish but missed the record by seven or eight pounds.

After the fish was lifted high for a triumphant photo and returned to the water, Anita flopped into the front deck chair, smiling from ear to ear, content to let all the adrenaline subside. But Ray knew that the northern were moving. It might be possible to get another as it came out of the shallow bay. He urged Clint to get his line back in the water as he quickly let his lure fall back to the proper depth.

The boat was in disarray after the fight with the monster, which had ranged all around the boat, but before he straightened up, Ray wanted a drink of his cup of coffee, which had miraculously avoided being spilled, and eat a bite of the butter twist which had been knocked over but amazingly landed frosted side up. He was halfway through the cup of coffee when he felt a mighty tug on his line and heard the scream of the drag. He started to arc the boat right but quickly realized the fish would require his full attention and shut the motor down. It felt big, even to him. He killed the engine and told Clint to reel in as he gingerly added a slight drag to the spool of his reel with his thumb. He finally stopped the progress of the fish and then had to reel his fastest to keep tension on the line as the fish made a dash directly towards the boat.

The fish swam past the boat then stripped line out against the drag in the other direction. As it passed, Ray knew this was a fish of a lifetime. It dwarfed even the behemoth that had just been released. With each pass, Ray revised his estimate upward, convinced that this fish might surpass the record by several pounds.

The safest strategy was to keep the fish swimming so that it would be truly exhausted before it came alongside the boat. Finally, Ray swam it alongside the left beam of the boat (he could never remember whether that was starboard or port). He was about to ask Clint to hand him the orange measuring stick from under the console when Anita, anticipating his request, picked the green one up from the floor where it lay and handed it to him.

<hr />

It is no exaggeration to say that he replayed the decision he made at that moment a thousand times in his head. But in the moment, what could he do? Try to confess and explain, risking his business and professional reputation with a record-breaking northern on the line? Or do what he did?

Even using the green ruler, the fish only missed the record by three-eighths of an inch, an estimated pound and a half. The accurate orange ruler would have easily put him in the record book. A framed eight-by-ten photo of the fish hangs in the center of his wall, but it must be said it brings him little pleasure. The picture frame is a bit more unusual. Though often asked about it, he has never told anyone its significance. It is made out of four pieces of a bright green ruler.

"For with what judgment you judge you will be judged;
and with the measure you use it will be measured back to you."

-Jesus

Have you given up judging others,
or do you keep that yardstick hidden away
for when you really need it.
No matter how well you have hidden it,
God knows where it is.
I hope you decide to get rid of it
before He uses it to measure you.

Nickels

Keith is four years old. He is the youngest son in a line of seven wonderful children my wife and I have. His oldest brother is married, so Keith has three nephews. The youngest, Emmitt, is two. Someday, two years difference will not be much, but right now, Keith is twice as old as his nephew, and he understands and has experienced many things Emmitt still has to learn.

Fortunately, my oldest son and his wife are moving a little closer to our home this summer, so let's imagine that as part of the move, Emmitt and his two brothers come to stay for a few weeks while my son and his wife get their new house ready for the family.

Keith loves playing with Emmitt, who follows him around, trying to do everything his uncle does. One afternoon, when they are playing in the house, I show up at the door with a stranger. The man, whom I have just met, was broken down on the side of the road. His car overheated, so I brought him to the house while his engine cooled to see if I had some anti-freeze for his radiator.

Keith and Emmitt meet me at the door, which is always a highlight for me. I give them big hugs and introduce them to the stranger, who I only know by his first name, Evan.

My son Keith has grown used to so many guests coming and going from our house, and he assumes that anyone who enters must have come to visit him. He starts telling Evan about his favorite topic, a trip to the zoo, which happened months before. It is old news around our house, but Keith realizes he has a new audience.

Evan is delighted to have this young man share his story. He listens with evident delight, and Emmitt, who has grown up with two older brothers, isn't shy about adding a comment wherever he can, whether it fits into the conversation or not. When I rejoin the group with a jug of anti-freeze, the gentleman is smiling broadly. He tells the boys he has to go, and then Evan looks up at me and asks if he can give them something. I nod, and he pulls out of his pocket the only thing he can find there. He has two nickels.

He hands one to each of the boys, who are both delighted. Emmitt has recently discovered his pockets, and a nickel is the perfect thing to put in a pocket. He puts his nickel in his pocket and runs off to show it to anyone he can find. Keith likes the feel of a nickel, too, but he knows that a nickel is worth something. He's not sure how much, but he knows that if he saves it up, someday he can go to the dollar store and get something cool. He runs to his room and puts the nickel in a safe place by his bed, where he keeps some money he is saving, as well as other treasures.

The next evening, we are all surprised by a knock at the door. The kids watch me as I go and answer it. When it opens, the youngest two immediately recognize Evan and come running over.

He has returned with a gallon of anti-freeze to replace the one I used on his car. I invite him in, thanking him sincerely for replacing it. I would never charge anyone for help, but knowing me, I would probably forget to replace the gallon of anti-freeze and never think of it again until I really needed it.

As he hands me the gallon jug, he sees the little boys looking up expectantly at him. Having almost forgotten the nickel incident, he reaches into his pocket to see if he has any change. Fishing out two dimes, he hands one to each of the boys.

They both thank him, as they have been taught, but Emmitt, in his two-year-old brain, is thinking, "What a gyp!" A dime is nowhere near as satisfying to hold in your pocket as a nickel. Keith, who is pretty perceptive for a four-year-old, runs to his stash and, grabbing the nickel from the day before, returns to offer Emmitt a trade.

Now they are both happy. Emmitt has a nickel in each pocket, and Keith has two dimes. He has learned that when he has ten dimes, he can go to the dollar store, so he puts the two dimes with his other treasures.

Meanwhile, I am taking a little more time to get to know Evan. We have a cup of tea together with my wife Mary and she asks him about his family. He tells us that he and his wife retired and moved into the area. They have children and grandchildren, but they all live far away, so the couple rarely gets to see them.

My wife immediately suggests he bring his wife for supper. He gladly accepts the invitation for the following evening.

Upon Evan's arrival with his wife, Mary Lou, the two youngest boys meet them at the door as usual. Evan excitedly introduces them to his wife and then presents them each with a new dollar bill.

Both boys politely express their thanks, but Emmitt is thinking, "This guy gets cheaper every day! Now, he is only giving me a scrap of paper."

Keith, on the other hand, knows that he now has enough to go shopping. He dreams of getting glow sticks, his favorite thing, at the dollar store, but when he sees Emmitt, he realizes his opportunity. He runs up to his room, sorts through his little stash of money, and finds two nickels.

Emmitt is happy to trade his dollar for two shiny nickels, and Keith is delighted that when he goes to the dollar store, he will be able to get glow sticks and a squirt gun.

The following week, I got a surprising phone call. It is Evan. The night that we shared supper, I got the impression that Evan and Mary Lou probably were rich by our standards. They didn't brag, but I picked up certain clues. Now Evan is calling seeking permission to give Keith and Emmitt each a check for ten thousand dollars to put in an account for college.

I protest, "That's very generous, but they don't need it."

Evan said, "Neither do a bunch of charities I give to, but my accountant insists that if I don't give it away the IRS will take it. I'd rather give it to the boys."

"Well, OK," I agree.

An hour or two later, Evan shows up at our door. I send Keith to open the door, and Emmitt trails behind him as usual. Both boys' faces brighten when they see their friend; by now, they have learned to expect something.

Evan doesn't disappoint them initially, he brings his hand from behind his back and hands each of the boys a ten-thousand-dollar check.

Now, even Keith shares Emmitt's opinion. "Really? A scrap of paper with some scribbling on it, and he expects me to be happy? He could have at least given me a nickel."

Paul described our God as being able to give us
"...above and beyond all we can ask or imagine."
When he offers you a gift beyond your understanding,
will you accept it with thanksgiving,
or demand a nickel?

Putterville

T he consensus of the people of Putterville was that the town was "behind the times, backward, simplistic, and regressive." Actually, this was only the consensus of those who were concerned about consensuses. The rest of the people thought it was a great town; some even thought it was the best town in the world. Even the people whose consensus was being consensitized liked the town enough to stay there.

If anyone asked them why they stayed in such a regressive, simplistic town, they were quick to point out that for them, it was OK, but one must think of the children.

You could have asked one of the children what they thought, but probably you couldn't have found a child to ask because they were all out at the swimming hole.

Now, if you were really interested in a consensus, that was one to take note of. All the kids loved the swimming hole. About a mile from the edge of town, the river tumbled over a ledge of rock, looped back on itself, and spread across a sandy bar. And best of all, twenty feet past the ledge, a big maple tree leaned out over the water. A thick hay rope had been tied to the highest branch by an earlier generation of Putterville kids. At the end of the rope was a big knot. And if you grabbed that knot and ran off the ledge, you could swing out to the middle of the bend where the water was deep.

All summer, the swimming hole was filled with Putterville children. From the time you were old enough to ride a bike until you had to get a job, summers meant days spent at the swimming hole. Generations of Putterville kids learned to swim in the swimming hole.

Even the kids in the nearby towns knew of the swimming hole. Many tried to find an excuse to come to Putterville in the summer to swim in the swimming hole.

The funny thing was that the swimming hole was one of the first things listed by the people who thought their town was regressive as evidence of just how backward the town was.

Euphilia Daphne Morgan-Schiller, who was convinced that her opinion was a primary contributor to the consensus of the town, put it this way: "It's disgraceful that our dear children must swim in an unsafe, unclean, disorganized, woefully unsupervised and ecologically fragile environment when all of the towns around have a swimming pool in which their children can safely interact with the water."

Although it wasn't particularly insightful or well said, it sounded *nuanced*, so it was often quoted by those who wanted to sound sophisticated.

The problem was that when Euphilia heard herself quoted, she assumed she was the new cultural influence in town. She began talking all the more about the "consensus" of the town, when in fact, none of it was fact.

By carefully limiting her sphere of friends to those who listened and believed her, she became more and more convinced that she spoke for the whole community. So she brazenly embarked upon the mission of dragging Putterville out of its backward, recalcitrant past into a progressive future, starting with getting a new swimming pool.

Now, it must not be supposed that Euphilia had any intention of actually helping to build the swimming pool, or to pay for the swimming pool, or to do anything else particularly useful. She believed that her job was to make the people of Putterville feel so bad about how backward they were, and how badly they were treating their children, that they would build a swimming pool and prove how right Euphilia was.

Her first plan was to get the children of Putterville to complain. She planned to have them go door to door with a petition for a new swimming pool, but when she tried to find some children to help her, they were nowhere to be found. Actually, they were somewhere; they were at the unsafe, unclean, disorganized, woefully unsupervised, and ecologically fragile swimming hole having a blast.

Now, if you can't find real kids to do your bidding, the next best thing is hypothetical children. Come to think of it, in many ways, hypothetical children are far superior to real children. Scientific studies have shown that hypothetical children conform to the results of scientific studies 87% more consistently than real kids. And that's what Euphilia needed, something she could count on.

Within weeks, her campaign was in full swing. Loaded with charts and graphs, she went to the town's bored meeting. Now, in Putterville, they were called "bored meetings" because nothing interesting had ever happened since fourteen years ago when Mayor Figdexter fell asleep while Secretary McWaddle was reading the minutes and dropped his... but that's a different story.

Today, things were going to be different. Euphilia had a dozen or so supporters there to plead the collective case of their hypothetical children, who were being left far behind in the march of progress because Putterville had no swimming pool. Each one stood up before the board and explained how, if they had children, they would want their children to have the opportunity of swimming in a public swimming pool and that they were confident that anyone who really cared about children as much as they cared about their hypothetical children, would be happy have a modest increase in their property taxes. They pointed out that they themselves would welcome such a modest increase, except that since their hypothetical children didn't actually need places to live, they all lived in apartments and wouldn't have to pay any increased taxes. Still, it was such a small price to pay "for the children."

All in all, that phrase "for the children" was worked into the evening so many times that by the time Euphilia sat down with her charts showing how study after study had conclusively proved that when people cared about the children, they were willing to spend money on studies proving that they really need to spend more money, the whole town board felt like they couldn't really turn down this request without looking like cold-hearted, ruthless, penny-pinching, snobs.

Their fate was sealed when J. Victor Carlson III spoke up. He asked why the swimming hole wasn't good enough for today's kids. "Why, when I was a kid, we all thought we were lucky to have the swimming hole." This was an excellent point, but since J. Victor Carlson III tended to be a cold-hearted, ruthless, penny-pinching snob, now everyone was sure they couldn't turn Euphilia down; after all, it was "for the children."

So it was that, at the beginning of the following summer, the town of Putterville had its own modern, clean, supervised, and progressive swimming pool. Everyone, even those opposed to the whole idea, couldn't avoid the infectious excitement of the new pool. The opening day was June first.

In the excitement, Euphilia had accepted a job as Summer Recreation Director. Normally, Euphilia liked to remain uninvolved so that she could retain her claim of being an objective cultural observer. But the excitement of the new pool and the prospect of being "In Charge" were too tempting.

Everyone agreed she deserved the job since she had been so instrumental in getting the pool and since she cared so much "for the children." Plus, anyone with real kids, instead of the hypothetical kind, knew the job would be no picnic.

She was busy getting everything ready for the grand opening when she realized that she would need to hire some lifeguards. She put an ad in the Putterville Picayune for lifeguards and then started writing an application. She got through "Name" and "Address" and "Why do you want to be a lifeguard?" and was about to write "How well do you swim?" when she realized how unfair that was. If she required that the lifeguards be able to swim, it would be discrimination. If kids didn't know how to swim, it wasn't their fault. They didn't have the opportunity to go to a fine swimming pool like this. And the only kids who did know how to swim had learned at that disgusting backward swimming hole.

How would it look to have them as lifeguards? Maybe she could hire lifeguards from other towns. But no one would like that since there were many good swimmers in town. Perhaps she could hire some of the kids who hadn't learned to swim at the swimming hole. But a non-swimming lifeguard couldn't save anyone. But a swimming lifeguard would only make all the others feel bad, and she couldn't contribute to low self-esteem.

Euphilia was in a quandary. There had to be a solution. She lay awake at night pondering the complexities of being a fair-minded, progressive, caring Summer Recreation Director living in the real world.

As every day passed, she grew more worried and confused. Then, suddenly, on the morning of May thirty-first, she woke up, sprang out of bed, and hurried to the pool. She had had an inspiration, the perfect solution to her problem.

June first dawned clear and beautiful. School was out, and typically, the kids of Putterville would be on their bikes racing each other to the swimming hole. But today, they were all waiting outside the Putterville Municipal Pool and Recreation Building. They were standing in something resembling a line, clothed in a rainbow assortment of swimming suits with their towels under their arms, waiting for the new pool to open at 9:30.

When Euphilia arrived at 9:25, the first thing that struck her was how noisy it was. Certainly, she cared about "the children," she would never want to repress their childish curiosity and creativity, but she did hope that they would quiet down before she had to let them into the pool. She snuck in the side door. Turned on all the lights and then marched resolutely to the front door. She opened the front door and a very noisy cheer went up from the crowd of kids.

Euphilia tried to quiet the crowd and finally, she succeeded. With a tentative and somewhat unruly quiet, she addressed the group, "Children, I am so happy you are here today…"

<hr />

She managed to get about two sentences into her finely crafted speech, designed to emphasize the import of this day when the noise again reached its full volume. Euphilia was beginning to wish she had more of the hypothetical children this pool had been designed for and fewer of the real kids standing in line waiting to fill her pool with noise, Noise, NOISE!

She abandoned her speech, gained some semblance of quiet, and went on to explain the rules. "No running, no pushing, no horseplay, no diving, no water fights, no chicken fights, no throwing, no wrestling, no loud noises, no whistling, no splashing, no shouting, no snapping towels, and most of all," she said with a smile, "Remember to have fun!"

"Now, before I let you in, I want you to meet the lifeguards," she continued. "Lifeguards, please step forward."

From the back of the crowd stepped three of the puniest, scrawniest kids in the whole town of Putterville. These were the kids who were always chosen last on the playground. Euphilia thought that was a barbaric custom—letting kids pick teams. The victims were children like these poor dears; they suffered from low self-esteem, and she could just imagine how encouraged they would be to be chosen as the new lifeguards. But they didn't look very encouraged as they marched to the front of the crowd, which had lately elbowed them to the back. They looked like they would just as soon find a hole and crawl into it.

The kids in the crowd began to protest, "They can't swim! They can't be lifeguards." Euphilia smiled to herself; this backward town was about to be shown that you could break the old stereotypes. You didn't have to have sleek, muscular lifeguards sitting in their tower, making everyone else feel like weaklings. Euphilia hated that. She was about to introduce this town to a much kinder, gentler approach; something everyone could feel good about.

So Euphilia, followed by the four mortally embarrassed lifeguards, followed by the hoards of noisy children, marched into the Putterville Municipal Pool and Recreation Building, down the hall, and into the shining new pool room. Finally, there was some quiet. Euphilia was smiling in her moment of triumph when one of the stunned children said, "Where's the water?"

Still smiling, Euphilia answered, "Children, as I tried to explain out front, you are about to be a part of a swimming experience that will nurture and feed your inner being. Traditionally, swimming has been full of fear, fear of the water, and fear of what others will think of you. But this pool will be different. It will be a pool where everyone can be equal and interact…"

She was interrupted by someone asking again, "But where's the water?"

"As you can see, the pool has two feet of water. As we all get comfortable with that amount, we will add more water. It will be much safer this way, and it will give some people a chance to work as lifeguards who might never have had a chance. And, best of all, no one will have to feel left out because we won't add any more water until everyone feels comfortable with the current level."

One of the quicker-witted kids added, "And, worst of all, we won't have any fun."

"Let us not have any of those negative, regressive attitudes," chided Euphilia, "Now' as soon as our lifeguards have handed you a life jacket, you may put it on and step into the water."

To the credit of the kids of Putterville, most of them tried to have fun in Euphilia's pool, but since everything that you could do to have fun in two feet of water broke one of the rules, the only thing louder than the noise of the children was the constant shrill of the lifeguard's whistles.

Euphilia was glad when the pool closed. She had never endured such noise. She was tempted to march right over to city hall and resign, but her pride wouldn't let her give up…yet. This was her pool. She would just do things differently tomorrow. First, she looked at the list of rules. Apparently, it was inadequate. What else could she add? Her first thought was, "Nothing." But somehow, the list must be faulty, so she added the following: No tickling, No flicking people with the straps of your life jacket, No poking, No throwing life jackets, No spitting, No loud laughing, No loud talking, No sudden movements, and No unnecessary noise.

Then she thought about getting the lifeguards louder whistles, but since her head was still ringing, she couldn't bring herself to do it.

As Euphilia climbed up a step ladder to retrieve one of the life jackets hanging from the lights, she hoped that tomorrow would be better.

It was. Early in the morning of the second of June, a long trail of bikes raced out to the edge of town to the unsafe, unclean, disorganized, woefully unsupervised, and ecologically fragile environment of the swimming hole.

At 9:30, Euphilia was delighted to see that waiting outside the Putterville Municipal Pool and Recreation Building were her four lifeguards and about a half dozen other kids whose parents had bought them season tickets to the pool as a cheap alternative to daycare.

It was almost quiet. Euphilia smiled to herself. This was how she had imagined it: sitting at her desk overlooking the children splashing merrily in the two feet of water. Why, in a day or two, they might be able to add another foot of water. Her musings were interrupted by a delegation of children at the door.

"We're bored."

Euphilia was truly surprised. You mean you don't want to swim?

"We do, but we're tired of wading. Couldn't you fill the pool up?"

"Well, not everyone is as talented as you, so we can't fill the pool until they are ready. Why don't I put in a nice video on swimming for you to watch while we wait for the others?"

"OK"

Things continued for a while like that. Each day, the handful of children who had been sentenced to a summer at the pool would be waiting for Euphilia, and they would hurry in to watch whatever videos she had brought for them that day. At first, Euphilia tried to limit them to videos about swimming, but gradually, she had to allow a wider selection, including any videos that included water in them, even if it was only in a glass. Then she found a video game called Virtual Olympics, which had a swimming game. So, all in all, the summer was going quite well for her. She sat in her office making the certificates of appreciation, recognition, and participation, which she printed out on her computer and handed out liberally to the children participating in summer rec. as part of her program to build self-esteem.

That August, she happily handed out diplomas to each of the participants of her summer recreation program and included with each a trophy, stating unequivocally that "the child holding this trophy is a really great person!!!"

But with the coming of Fall, a new challenge was waiting for Euphilia. Elmer Gooch, known better around town as "Coach" since he had been coaching football for the Putterville Pirates for as long as anyone could remember, was waiting for Euphilia when she came to work one morning.

"You better not have any ideas of getting any of my boys to join your swim team. They've been working real good together and we've got us a shot at the regional championship this year. I need all those boys, and I don't need someone recruitin' 'em for the swim team."

Euphilia was speechless. How dare this ruffian threaten her? But, why did he think she would even want to have a swim team? None of the kids could swim. She couldn't possibly have a swim team. But how dare he tell her that? She tried to splutter out an answer. The words wouldn't come. Puzzled, Coach walked out. From what he had heard, he expected more of a fight. She'd just stood there. Oh, well.

When he was gone, Euphilia regained enough composure to pull out her contract and re-read it. There it was in her contract. She was expected to coach the swim team. She, Euphilia Daphne Morgan-Schiller, was expected to coach a team and...ugh...

compete. Well, she would have to get out of it. There was no way; she couldn't even swim. She marched over to city hall and straight into the Mayor's office.

"I can't do it," she said

"Do what?" the Mayor asked.

"Someone put a line in my contract about being the swimming coach. I won't do it. I will not support anything so vile and destructive as making children compete. The angels should never have to suffer that."

"Now see here," said the Mayor, "we built that white elephant just to make you happy. The kids didn't want it. The people didn't want it. No one wanted it. But now that we've got it, we're gonna use it. All the towns around us have swimming pools like you pointed out, and they've been calling us backward and old-fashioned like you pointed out. Now, we may be backward and old-fashioned, but I will wager my last dollar that nobody swims better than the kids of Putterville."

Euphilia was at the point of tears, "But, I can't even swim."

"You don't need to," the Mayor answered, "just put these kids in the water, and they'll swim circles around the competition. I watch them swimming every day when I drive home from work. They're good, and now that we have a pool, we can prove to the world."

Euphilia was aghast, "You don't mean the ruffians at the swimming hole! Those children are noisy and disrespectful, and besides, they haven't even come to the pool all summer. You can't possibly mean for me to have them on the team."

"I don't care who is on your team or how you run it, but you will coach a swim team, and it had better be good enough to put those other schools in their place."

"But, it's a matter of principle with me," Euphilia made one last protest.

"It is with me, too. We've put up with your nonsense long enough. Now, get!" The mayor dismissed Euphilia.

Euphilia walked back to her office. How could this be happening to her? She had done so much for the children, especially the ones in her program. She had worked so hard to nurture their self-esteem; every day, she carefully chose the videos they watched to make sure they supported tolerance and diversity. Why, she had used up three reams of paper just printing certificates. And now her poor dears were going to be overrun by a bunch of thugs who got to be on the team just because they could swim fast. She wouldn't do it. "The mayor said he didn't care who was on the team," thought Euphilia, "I'll have a team that cares about something besides winning."

Euphilia went to the office and called her four lifeguards and the six participants in summer rec. and asked them to come to a special meeting.

When the meeting was held, she addressed the group. "You have each been selected for a very great honor because you are special and because you have been participating in our summer recreation program. You have the opportunity to represent the town of Putterville on the swim team.

"What! Us?" one of the lifeguards named Ann said. "We could never win. Besides, none of us know how to swim."

"You know winning isn't everything." Euphilia countered.

"But it is something," Ann responded. "Don't you think we look stupid enough as the only non-swimming lifeguards in the world without forcing us to make fools of ourselves in front of a crowd? I hate this job. I'm only here because it's the only way to get paid to watch videos."

"Ditto here," said a boy named Sam, whose parents were very successful business people, "I don't want to be on a swim team. My parents dump me off here when they're at work. I would have complained more, but once you brought in the video game, we just hid your lame games and played something cool."

"We haven't learned anything all summer," said Jake, another one of the lifeguards. "When I was offered a job as a lifeguard, I was excited. I always wanted to be a lifeguard but needed to work on my swimming. I thought I would get a chance. But the way you run things, no one gets a chance. With a little help, I could be a real lifeguard, but it'll never happen here. Here, we'll always be a bunch of losers."

Euphilia couldn't believe it. These children were just as hopeless as the rest of the little beasts. Oh, why couldn't she reside in a town where there were normal, beautiful children? But, she needed them on the team, whatever it took.

So she started crying. Here, she was just trying to make the world a fairer place to give everybody an equal chance. And the very people she had helped the most were turning against her. Didn't they know that they owed it to her to be proud of being losers? The world needed to see more proud losers, or else nothing would ever change. The world would continue to be run by winners. They had an obligation to show the world that they stood for something. Being on her team was their chance.

Now, nothing gives children the feeling of power more than having someone try to manipulate their emotions. They could get anything from this crazy lady. Let the good times roll!

The first offer came from a kid named Sam. "I might be on the team, He said, "but my mom always has fresh caramel rolls waiting for me when I get home from school. I'd hate to miss that."

"Well, we could have a treat every day before practice."

"Not some stale cookies from a package!"

"Oh no, I'll bake fresh cookies daily," Euphilia promised.

Another kid joined the bargaining, "Well, I might be on the team, but usually my dad brings me new video games to play after school.

"I could bring video games…"

Had Euphilia not been so desperate, she might have been skeptical that the same parents who abandoned their kids for a whole summer with her, baked fresh caramel rolls, brought their children new video games every night, did their homework for them, took them out for pizza twice a week, or took them to an amusement park every weekend. But desperate didn't even begin to describe Euphilia. She needed them. "Not that having these greedy losers on her team would help much," she thought. "Oh, why? Why? Couldn't she work with normal angelic children like she always read about?"

The first day of practice went well. The children were quiet while they ate the fresh cookies and played the video games Euphilia brought, which gave her time to finish most of their homework. When the cookies were eaten and the last of the algebra was finished, Jake said, "Don't you think we should at least practice swimming?"

"What?" Euphilia cried, "And give them the satisfaction of forcing you into their contemptible mold of competition. No, I am proud of you just the way you are." (Which wasn't strictly the truth, but she didn't think it would build their self-esteem to tell them, "Practice or not, you losers couldn't beat anyone.")

So, after a week of cookies, pizza, and video games, it was time for the first swim meet. It was to be sponsored by Putterville to show off their new pool, and it was called the "Putterville Invitational," which Euphilia thought made it sound "warm and friendly," the kind of gathering that might be accepting of her new ideas.

They weren't. When the opposing teams arrived, they immediately started complaining about the water level.

"Someone had better get some water in here now. "The coach of the Milton Marauders yelled.

"Now, three feet is plenty to swim in, and we don't want to discriminate against those who can't swim."

"Can't SWIM!! This is a swim meet.??!!" queried the Coach of the Danburg Destroyers

"I know, but I've always felt it is important to be inclusive. Some of my team can't swim yet, but they are still welcome on my team."

"Lookit, lady, the rules say the pool has to have water in it to have a swim meet. So you can either forfeit this meet or fill the pool and issue your team life jackets," said the coach of the Westbrook Warriors, with intended sarcasm.

But as fate would have it, that was the moment the Putterville Pirates made their grand entrance, wearing their bright orange life jackets.

———

By nine o'clock that night, the Mayor had finally calmed down enough to talk reasonably to Euphilia. She answered on the eleventh ring.

"Ms. Morgan 'Hyphen' Schiller?"

"Yes," she answered meekly.

"Listen and listen carefully. Tomorrow, I will have ten kids who know how to swim at your practice. You will have the pool filled and waiting for them. You will be the coach, but I will run practices my way. And above all, YOU WILL NOT FORCE THEM TO WEAR LIFE JACKETS! Do you understand me?"

He had to imagine the nodded answer.

———

Euphilia thought several times about running away, but she didn't know where she would go. She didn't have any fundamental skills; only a town like Putterville was kind enough to put up with the eccentricities of a busybody like her. Anywhere else, they lock up people like her as a public nuisance, or even worse, just ignore them. She would have to go through with it.

The next day, the pool was filled and ready. The Mayor stormed in at three o'clock and just glared at Euphilia. Ten minutes later, the team filed out of the locker room. One tanned, muscular body after another. Just like all the stereotypes. Euphilia couldn't contain her disdain. "Mister Mayor, I see that you couldn't get beyond the prejudices and stereotypes that I have worked so hard to combat. Did it ever occur to you that someone besides the tanned muscular swimmer type might want to be on the team?"

"Did it ever occur to you that they got tanned and muscular because they have been swimming all summer? Where do you think I found these kids? I've been watching them swim at the swimming hole all summer."

The team lined up, but when the Mayor counted, there were eleven on the team. Down at the end, fighting down embarrassment, stood Jake, the scrawny lifeguard. Euphilia rushed over and tried to whisper, "Jake, didn't you get the message? There's a new swim team."

"I know," He whispered back.

Euphilia tried again, "You can't be on the team anymore, the Mayor's in charge." The one thing Jake wanted was to slip in unnoticed, and suddenly, all eyes were on him, thanks to this deranged lunatic.

"Look! It's the lifeguard!" someone shouted, and everyone broke out laughing. The Mayor strolled over like a drill sergeant. Jake was shaking.

"Son, you don't have to be here; we've got real lifeguards now."

"Can I stay?" Jake trembled.

"Do You want to?"

"Do I want to!" Jake's anger bolstered his courage, "I've come to this pool every day since it has been opened. Why? Because I want to swim. But no one would teach me. I have had excuses made for me. I've had certificates given to me. I've even been getting paid to be able to swim, but no one has taught me how to swim or even let me into water above my head. Doesn't anyone believe I can learn how to swim?"

Jake looked around. He'd hardly ever spoken a word in public before, and now, he had the Mayor of Putterville, the swim team, two janitors, and Euphilia all staring at him. He exhaled and turned to slink back to the locker room.

"Hey, where are you going?" It was the Mayor's voice... "You just made the swim team."

Skeeter

S keeter was seven years old when he planted his first garden. He planted it in a clearing in the woods behind his house. Every day, he carried water from the pump and pulled up the weeds in the little space he had dug up. Finally, he started to see little green shoots coming up in the row he had planted. Every day, they got bigger, and Skeeter got more excited. One Sunday near the end of June, when his grandparents came for a visit, Skeeter took his grandfather out to the garden. With pride, he showed off his garden and the tender green plants, which were almost up to his knees. He could tell that Grandfather was pleased. Grandfather was one of the wisest men in the village, and Skeeter was pretty sure that he knew everything.

Grandfather looked at the garden and noticed how all the weeds had been pulled out. Then he took a handful of the dirt, crumbled it in his hands, and sniffed it. "You've got some real nice soil here, Skeeter, "Grandfather commented, "plenty of organic material but with enough sand to drain well. You picked a good spot here too; you get nice sun during the morning but enough shade in the afternoon to keep from scorching your plants." Then, with a puzzled look, he asked, "What are you growing? It looks like milkweed."

"It is," Skeeter replied

"Why are you growing milkweed Skeeter?"

"Don't you remember last fall? I found all those green pods at your house. When I opened them, they had those things that looked like fish with brown scales." Grandfather began to nod in remembrance as Skeeter continued, "When I asked you what they were, you told me they were milkweed pods, and you showed me how each scale had white fluff so it would float on the wind. Then you told me that if I took one of those seeds and planted it, it would grow into a milkweed plant."

"Well, it sure looks like it is working," Grandfather said, looking serious but very proud of his grandson. "How many plants do you have there?"

"Fifteen," Skeeter responded proudly.

"Well, if you take care of them, you should get a bunch of milkweed pods." After that, every time Grandfather visited, he went with Skeeter to see his milkweed patch, and when August came he helped his grandson proudly collect two baskets full of milkweed pods.

"What are you going to do with them?" Grandfather asked, "Because if you don't need them all, I'd like to buy a basket full."

"What will you use them for?" Skeeter asked.

"Oh…. I figure they might be handy to have around someday. The only problem is I don't have any money now, but I could pay you later."

"Grandfather! You can have a basket of them." Skeeter offered.

Grandfather took one of the baskets and carried it to his car. Skeeter felt like a grown-up when Grandfather shook his hand and said, "That's very kind of you, I won't forget."

But Skeeter forgot, fall came, and he spent day's ricing, then it was time to hunt. Skeeter didn't get to hunt yet, but if he worked hard and had all of his kindling split, his father would take him out to the woods to sit with him while he hunted. Then the snow came, and then Christmas. There were so many exciting things that Skeeter seldom thought about his garden. Still, sometimes he would dream about the next summer and making a bigger garden. Nobody except Grandfather had wanted any milkweed pods, but next year, he would plant enough to give his grandfather three or four baskets.

Then, one day in February, his grandparents came to visit. After dinner, Grandfather took Skeeter aside and said, "I guess it's time to settle up. I owe you some money for the milkweed last summer.

"Oh, Grandfather, you don't have to pay me," said Skeeter. "I'm glad you wanted them... no one else did."

"No, I promised to pay you," Grandfather said, and he pulled a crisp dollar bill out of his breast pocket. Now, in those days, a dollar was something. Maybe you can imagine how much it was worth, if I tell you that a candy bar only cost a nickel. If I do my math right, that means Skeeter was holding in his hands enough money for twenty candy bars. Skeeter was already dreaming about his next trip to the store when Grandfather interrupted him. "I brought you this catalog too," he said. "I got an extra copy and didn't want it to go to waste. Now you run along and find a safe place for that money."

Skeeter ran up to the little upstairs room he shared with his brothers and pulled a box his father had made him from under the bed. He set it beside him on the bed and put the dollar safely into the box with his other treasures, still thinking about the candy he could buy. He was going to put the catalog into the box, too, but he decided he would look at it first. It was a seed catalog.

Every page was filled with drawings and descriptions of vegetables and flowers. Skeeter hadn't been able to read very long, so he sounded out the long words and read about delicious green beans guaranteed to produce many bushels from each plant, huge juicy tomatoes that would be ready by the end of July, cabbage that would grow so big only one would fit in a wheelbarrow, and corn that was so sweet and tender it would be the envy of all your neighbors.

Skeeter lay there in the bed reading the catalog until he was called down to supper. As he climbed down the stairs, he was not dreaming of candy bars, but of seeds, he was going to buy for his garden.

The following week, he took his dollar to school and asked his teacher to help him place the order. It cost nineteen cents for a stamp and return postage, leaving him eighty-one cents for early giant tomatoes, Golden sweetie corn, regal boy greens beans, tall Tom carrots, and a package of summer crisp kohlrabi. Skeeter had no idea what kohlrabi was, but it was the only thing in the whole catalog for seven cents, which was all he had left of Grandfather's dollar. For six cents, he could have gotten a surprise package of mixed flowers, but he didn't think it was right to come out a penny under.

The seeds came in plenty of time for planting, and that was the longest spring he could remember. The catalog said that the earliest planting time for his area was May seventeenth, and that year, the seventeenth of May took even longer than Christmas to arrive.

Skeeter planted his garden and tended it carefully, weeding it twice a week and carrying water from the pump every day. By July, he was picking beans, and nothing had ever tasted so good to him. Every week, more produce came into season, and he was feeding his family, his grandparents, and many neighbors.

Skeeter was hooked. He loved gardening, and each year, his garden was bigger and better. Soon, he had a reputation for the best garden in the village. People encouraged him to set up a stand to sell the vegetables, but Skeeter asked, "Why? I can always grow more." He shared with everyone he knew. His mother would have enough for the family to eat all winter, but there were always plenty of extra vegetables.

Skeeter grew up and married Ellen, the most beautiful girl in the village (at least he thought so), and they began a family. He was busy providing for his new family, but he never outgrew his love of gardening. Now, with more mouths to feed, it was more important than ever. Each spring, he started the little plants in his windowsill, watching and waiting until he thought the weather was warm enough to move them outside. Then, he would carefully tend to the small plants and add rows of other seeds, watching over the garden carefully and watering it regularly when the rains didn't fall. Skeeter would grow some of everything. Beans, corn, tomatoes, carrots, beets, cucumbers, squash, pumpkins, cabbage, peas, radishes, lettuce, Brussels sprouts, asparagus, broccoli, spinach, cauliflower, parsnips, turnips, and kohlrabi, which, after his first year, he found out he liked.

Not everything would grow well every year. Some years were too cold for the tomatoes or too dry for the cabbage. Some years, there were too many bugs for the cauliflower or too much sun for the peas. And sometimes the deer or the rabbits or some other animal would get into the garden and eat some of the vegetables before they were ripe. But other crops made up the difference, and Skeeter's new family always had plenty to eat. As his children grew up, they all had to help in the garden.

Actually, they had to help with lots more than the garden. In those days, parents weren't afraid to make their kids work. They figured, "Hard work never hurt me, so it won't hurt my kids." So, just like their parents had made them do, Skeeter and Ellen's children had to help plant, weed, water, and harvest the garden, help feed the chickens and gather the eggs, help pick raspberries, blueberries, June berries, choke cherries, pin cherries, and cranberries, and help Ellen store them for winter. They had to help stomp and winnow the wild rice that Skeeter and his brother, Uncle Suds, would bring home in the fall; then, they would have to watch it carefully over the fire while they stirred it and enjoyed the rich smell of the parching rice. When the rice was all parched and stored, it was time to help get the wood cut before hunting season started, and the lakes froze hard enough to set the nets.

But as the children grew up working hard, Skeeter noticed that his third son Ivan (who everybody called Cobbie) had inherited his love of gardening. Even after a day of hard work, Cobbie would always walk out to the garden with his dad in the evenings to see how the plants were coming. Maybe the reason Cobbie liked the garden so well was that he loved corn on the cob. Even as a baby, before he had teeth, they would give him a corn cob from the table, and he would gnaw on it until every last bit of corn was gone, then ask for another. That was where his nickname came from. One day, when he was three, his brothers convinced their mother to let him eat as many ears of corn as he could. He quit halfway through the sixth cob, but half an hour after supper was done, he came back and ate the rest of that cob and asked for another.

Whether it was because he loved corn or because he loved gardening, each year, he took on more responsibility in the garden. He would watch all of the plants carefully and nurture them in any way possible, but none more lovingly than the corn. The year Cobbie turned ten, they had the biggest corn patch ever. He had convinced his father to buy three different varieties of corn so that they could have some early, some at the usual time, and some late. That way, Cobbie hoped to have corn on the cob from early August until the beginning of October. Twice a week, he hoed the corn patch and watched it grow. The early corn wasn't very tall, but by the second week in July, he could already feel the small ears of corn growing inside their husks. Almost every day, he felt them to see how quickly they were growing. He couldn't wait until they could have their first meal of corn on the cob.

On July twenty-fourth, Cobbie decided that the corn would be ready in two more days, but someone else was watching the corn.

The next morning, when Cobbie and his dad went out to hoe the garden, Cobbie looked at the patch and felt like crying. Every ear of corn in the early rows had been broken off and eaten. The empty cobs were lying strewn about. Skeeter pointed down by his son's feet and said, "Bandits!"

They knelt down to look, and there, in the loose soil, were raccoon tracks. Everywhere! There must have been at least a dozen raccoons that came and ate every single ear. But with their raccoon cleverness, they didn't touch any of the green ears in the other rows. That, at least, was some consolation for Cobbie. He figured it just meant waiting another two weeks for the next rows of corn to get ripe.

Several days before those rows were ripe, Cobbie woke to find that the bandits had returned. They had stripped anything even close to being ripe from the stalks and left half-eaten cobs lying throughout the garden. Cobbie was furious. He hadn't even worried about them returning; he should have known better. Now, the only corn left was two rows of later-ripening corn. Cobbie vowed that he wouldn't let the four-legged bandits get the last of his corn. But he didn't know what to do.

He decided he would sleep out by the garden. The weather was still nice, and the fall rains had not begun yet. That night, Cobbie brought an old blanket down by the corn patch. He gathered several armloads of grass from the ditch and made a comfortable bed for himself. He sank back into the straw heap and fell asleep right away, but that first night, he was awakened by every noise. Every one of the village dogs that walked through the yard, every owl that hooted, and every coyote that howled out in the Buckboard hills woke Cobbie up, which pleased him. Surely, he would hear the bandits if they came again.

But anyone who has spent time in the woods knows that the sounds of the night quickly become as commonplace as the sounds of a house. It took only two or three nights for Cobbie to be as comfortable with the howling coyotes as he was with his brother Sammy's snoring. Soon, he was sleeping the night through the way most hard-working boys do. This was why, even though the raccoons passed within 4 feet of where Cobbie was sleeping, he never heard them until they had almost finished eating the last rows of corn. One of the raccoons, who had already had his fill of fresh corn, started exploring the garden. The watering can was hanging upside down on a post at the edge of the garden. The raccoon climbed the post and stuck his head into the hole beside the post to lick the few drops of water caught on the rim of the watering can. Unfortunately, the hole was the perfect size to let the head in but not to let it out again. The raccoon started fighting against the can and thrashing around, tipping the post, which was not stuck too deeply in the ground.

The raccoon was backing all around the garden, trying to shake loose the can, making such a racket that Cobbie woke up. It took him a minute to realize what had awakened him, but when he finally realized what was happening, he jumped up and started chasing the raccoons out of the garden.

Despite his planning, the stick he had kept next to him when he first began sleeping out had been misplaced. Cobbie was so angry he didn't care. He ran after the raccoons who were waddling away, their stomachs stuffed full of corn. Whenever he caught up to one, he gave it as hard a kick as his bare feet would allow. The smaller raccoons would roll head over heels, get up, and waddle on their way.

The raccoon in the watering can had finally worked his head loose and ran for the woods, but not before leaving the post right where Cobbie tripped over it when he walked back to see if anything was left of his corn patch.

All the corn was gone. But there were plenty of other vegetables, as Skeeter and Ellen pointed out to Cobbie the next morning. There would be enough to eat for that winter. Even if they didn't get corn, they would be OK. It didn't console Cobbie. He wasn't about to forget that the four-legged furry bandits had taken his favorite vegetable. He vowed he wouldn't let it happen again.

During the winter, Cobbie asked everyone he knew who had a garden how they kept raccoons out of their garden. Most told him. "Just plant plenty; some years they come, and some years they don't." But that wasn't good enough for Cobbie. He didn't want to put all that effort into a garden if he wasn't going to get lots of corn on the cob in the fall. Some people had other suggestions: scarecrows, noisemakers, traps, and scents. The next year, Cobbie's garden looked like a cross between the midway at the fair and a junkyard. He tried every suggestion. He had scarecrows and pinwheels, Cans hanging from branches, and streamers tied to the corn stalks. He planted marigolds and carried bales of hair from the barber in town to spread around his corn patch in hopes of foiling the midnight bandits.

But again, they found his corn and destroyed more than half of the patch.

———————

There was a reason why. You see, living out there in the village, there were often chances to get a baby raccoon, and almost every family at one time or another had kept one as a pet. They were so cute and seemed so harmless and playful that few could resist their charms or the begging of the children who wanted to keep one as a pet. Eventually, the little bandits would get so big that the parents in the home would insist that something had to be done. But after living with the family for that long, few fathers had the resolve to carry out their threat to shoot them; instead, they would be convinced just to take the raccoons out into the woods so they could return to their wild ways.

These raccoons combined their knowledge of the world of men with their new freedoms and became cunning and fearless bandits. Cobbie's wasn't the only garden they visited. Even a latch couldn't keep them out if they thought there was food to be found inside a gate, a shed, or even a house. The dogs in the village had learned to give the coons a wide berth, partly because they weren't allowed to hurt the ones that were kept as pets and partly because once the raccoons had grown to a full size, they could make things unpleasant for any, but the biggest dogs.

That fall, Cobbie saved every penny he could earn, and the following spring, he purchased a dog. No one in the village ever bought a dog. You might possibly trade something for a particularly smart or good-looking dog from a neighbor, but dogs were just a fact of life. There were always plenty of them and always neighbors with a new litter of puppies who were only too happy to get rid of one. But that wasn't good enough for Cobbie. He earned forty-seven dollars, enough money to buy a black and tan puppy from a kennel down in St. Cloud.

That summer, Cobbie's garden wasn't as nice as usual – the weeds were much larger, and the vegetables looked like they hadn't been watered very often. Even the corn, Cobbie's favorite, was somewhat neglected. For one thing, Cobbie figured it wasn't worth the effort to keep trying if the four-legged thieves carried it all away. In addition, Cobbie was spending all his time with his new dog. He read every book he could find on the subject of coon dogs, and Cobbie was determined that his dog would solve the raccoon problem.

Unfortunately, the dog was still a pup and couldn't be expected to hunt well until he was at least a year old. Cobbie could hardly wait. He pictured himself running the dog through the woods, bringing to bay all the raccoons guilty of raiding his corn patch. Then, once they were brought to justice, he would show everyone. His garden would have the biggest, juiciest corn on the cob. In his daydreams, he could almost imagine the warm butter dripping down his arms as he bit into a sweet, juicy cob of corn.

<hr />

The next summer, Cobbie and his Dad planted another big garden. Skeeter no longer worked in the woods; he had a job in town, so he wasn't there to tend the garden. He counted on Cobbie to do that, but somehow, Cobbie was spending most of his time trying to teach the dog to hunt.

Maybe the problem was that the raccoons were unusually smart, many of them having been brought up among people, or maybe Cobbie's dog wasn't that good of a hunter, but it seemed like the raccoons were always a step ahead of him. Almost every night, he was out trying to tree a coon, but only twice did he succeed. Staying out every night sure took away his incentive to work on the garden, plus Cobbie figured if he couldn't get rid of many raccoons before the corn got ripe, there was no real reason to try. So, the garden became more and more overgrown with weeds. Even the crops that always had plenty, like the green beans and the zucchini squash, were hardly producing enough for Cobbie's family, let alone enough to share with the neighbors like they always used to do. Cobbie began to think he could never win his little war against the raccoons.

Skeeter's Grandfather was very old by this time. Grandmother had passed away, and Grandfather had gone to live with his daughter down in Minneapolis. She assured him that she could take much better care of him down there in her home, and she was probably right, but He didn't like it much. The paved streets and the mowed yards were not the kind of world he loved, so on his 90th birthday, he made an announcement. "I'm going back home. Maybe I can live longer here with your wonderful care, but I want to be home." Something about the look in his eye convinced Skeeter's sister that there was no arguing this time. She placed a long-distance call to Skeeter, who said, of course, Grandfather could live with them.

Everything was a bustle at Cobbie's home that week. They had to rearrange rooms so that his great-grandfather could have his own room. This meant that Cobbie and his brothers would stay in the shed, which was pretty exciting for them. It would be cold come winter, but they could stand it, and staying in the shed promised to be an adventure. They spent the week cleaning and moving, and on Saturday afternoon, when Cobbie's Aunt and Uncle brought their family and Grandfather, everyone was excited.

The weekend was spent with lots of relatives coming by to visit. Cobbie didn't know he had so many cousins, but it was fun playing softball and kick the can in the backyard with them all.

Sunday night, everyone packed up and left. When Cobbie came down for breakfast Monday morning, Grandfather was waiting for him. "Good morning, sleepy head. I wondered when you would get up. I heard you have a garden, and I thought you'd better take me out to see it."

Cobbie was surprised at how talkative Grandfather was. When everyone was around yesterday, he had hardly said a word. "OK, Grandfather. But, can you make it out there?"

"Hmph" Grandfather looked disdainful. "First, they pave everything with concrete and blacktop, then they make you carry a cane so you don't fall down. There's nothing that will hurt me out there in that garden... except that ferocious-looking dog of yours. Looks like a coon dog. Reminds me of a dog my brother had..."

Grandpa told stories while Cobbie ate his cornflakes, and then they went out to see the garden. It looked pretty bad, and Cobbie felt ashamed of how he'd let the weeds grow up. Grandpa seemed not to notice. He pointed to the tattered remains of a scarecrow hanging from a pole in the garden. "Who's that? he asked, "Anyone I know?"

Cobbie told him the story of all he had done in his attempt to thwart the bandits. He showed Grandfather all of the noisemakers and traps he had laid. He told about all the nights of hunting and how impossible it all seemed." He liked his grandfather and hoped maybe he could tell him how to defeat the raccoons.

Grandfather found a bucket, turned it over, sat down, and surveyed the garden. He looked at the dog carefully then he turned and asked Cobbie, "Would you like to know what your problem is?"

"Yes, Grandfather, I would."

"Well, it looks to me like you have spent too much time hating the raccoons and not enough time growing your garden. You see, Cobbie, Raccoons aren't the only things that will eat your garden; sometimes it will be bugs, sometimes your garden will get wrecked by a storm, and sometimes you get a late frost in the spring or an early freeze in the fall. But none of those things can stop you if you keep on growing. When you get angry at the raccoons or the bugs or the weather, pretty soon, you will start feeling sorry for yourself. Then you will forget about growing anything, and the only thing you will have to pass on to your family and neighbors will be a harvest of anger and self-pity."

"But do you mean I should just let the raccoons eat everything I worked so hard for?"

"Absolutely not! You should do everything that you can to stop the raccoons…except hate them!

"If you spent your whole summer growing corn just to feed it to the raccoons, you would have earned my respect. But if, in your anger or self-pity, you quit growing a garden because they might steal it, you will never earn anyone's respect, not even your own," Grandpa finished slowly, getting up from the bucket he was sitting on. "Now, how about you haul some water from the pump while I start pulling out some weeds."

Grandfather passed away the next spring. The night after they buried him, Cobbie woke up in the middle of the night. He thought he heard something in the garden, so he looked out the window. He saw his father, Skeeter, sitting in the garden crying. Cobbie went out to him, and all the sadness he had been trying to keep inside himself came running out in tears. They both cried quietly for a long time. Then Skeeter told Cobbie the story of his first garden of milkweed and how Grandfather had taught him to love gardening. Cobbie told his father about their talk the previous summer, and there, in the moonlit night, the two of them started planning their next garden. It was the best ever.

Authors Note: Mom was probably the biggest fan of my stories. I had the honor of conducting her funeral when she passed away after a long struggle with ALS (Lou Gehrig's disease). For months, maybe years, before her death, she had been trying to choose which of her favorite stories to have me tell for her funeral. Finally, she gave up and left the choice to me. The following is the story I told. It represents the choice my Mother made throughout her life to seek out the most needy and to share with them the love she had found in Jesus.

Guests of Honor

When Abner married Katy, he took her to live as far up into the mountains as it was possible to live. You could survive higher up, but only with what you carried with you. As often as Abner could, he would climb the higher reaches, but their farm was the highest up in the mountains of any of his neighbors, and for the most part, he and Katy were self-sufficient, only rarely needing to go down the mountain to get supplies.

One of the reasons Abner chose to live there was reinforced every time he made a trip down to the town. Journeying to the valley was like taking a trip in a time machine. The mountains still were the domain of horses. But down in the valley, the world was filling with all kinds of new contraptions. First, the train came, which connected the far-flung parts of the new nation. Abner accepted it as a blessing of sorts and even took a trip with Katy. But now there were all sorts of other vehicles scurrying in every direction, as if, with the new technology, everyone had been infected with an irrational need to hurry. Cars, trucks, motorcycles, and tractors all plied an increasing maze of hard-packed roads that covered the old trails. Abner had been tempted for a while by the usefulness of a tractor but quickly realized it would only make him need to travel to town more often to get fuel, which would probably require a truck. He wondered if the primary role of technology was to make you need more. He couldn't imagine the world his son Jack would inherit, but for now, he would live in the time warp the mountains created.

The mountains also preserved the quality of the neighborhood. For one thing, the top edge of their property had nothing but mountainous wilderness, and the neighbors further down were all people who daily had the reminder that character was a superior commodity to comfort. Whatever innovations the march of time brought might make character optional, but it would never make it obsolete. Abner and Katy discussed it often; they wouldn't fight the changes that were descending upon them, but they would prepare for them by raising their son in an environment requiring strength, determination, and courage, trusting that it would equip him to meet the onslaught of a world of convenience with its inherent weakness.

One day, on a trip to town, Abner met with some of their older former neighbors whose health kept them in the valley but whose hearts were in the mountains. They had startling news. The Mountains were going to be made into a national park. Some forward-thinking individuals in our country's distant capital decided that our country should set aside a region of the mountains and protect it from the people who understood it best, making it the property of the national community. They wanted to develop an infrastructure that would allow people from all over the country who had never had a chance to interact with mountains to come and experience firsthand a national treasure.

As the men of the mountains discussed the idea, it was clear that their opposition wasn't just a natural dislike of change. They had a clear objection: the new infrastructure would allow people from all over the country, who had never had a chance to interact with mountains, to come and experience firsthand how many ways a mountain could kill you.

The people far from the mountains failed to realize that mountains teach people character by killing those who don't have it. The thought of paving a highway up to the heart of the mountains so that people could drive their comfortable new sedan to a fierce and unforgiving land without any cautionary hardship en route seemed foolish, but by the time the news reached their small town, the decisions had, for all practical purposes, been made.

Abner returned to the family with a heart heavy with concern and told the family the news. Abner's fears weren't just for the status of his property but for those who would come to visit. As they talked, it seemed useless to oppose the decision: what would their voice mean even if they could somehow make it heard? People just didn't understand the mountains. Katy, trying to console her husband, offered, "Maybe they will get someone who understands the mountains to run the park."

At that moment, Abner realized there was something he could do. Even though the decision-makers lacked the common sense to realize the implications of what they were doing, maybe they could recognize common sense when they saw it in person. The next day, Abner journeyed to the town again to collect every scrap of information he could find on the new project. He focused on the names and addresses of people involved in the project. Armed with this list and several boxes of envelopes from the general store, he returned home. With Katy's help and Jack licking the envelopes and the stamps, they wrote to everyone they could think of connected to the project, including the president, asking for Abner to be made the park's ranger.

Most of the letters were ignored, but Abner received enough responses to get a sense of who would be making the decision about the head of the new park. He redoubled his efforts, writing as often as he had a new thought about the advisability of having someone who knew the mountains run the park. He encouraged the neighbors who understood his concerns to write, too. Finally, he made the trip to the capital to knock on doors. After two weeks in the city and hours of waiting, he returned home triumphantly with a new title. He was the new Park Ranger.

The following summer, work began on the park in earnest. The first major obstacle was making a decent road up to the area chosen for the park headquarters. Abner watched as they blasted and bulldozed the path into the mountains and was impressed but apprehensive about the nice, smooth surface they produced.

The headquarters buildings were quickly erected, and it seemed like a constant stream of traffic hauled materials and workers into a part of the mountain that had previously been visited only on foot or on horseback.

Abner, Katy, and Jack moved into the newly built Park Ranger's residence, and shortly thereafter, with great fanfare, the park was declared open. Many of the politicians and bureaucrats Abner had met in D.C. were on hand. When they saw the surrounding mountains, they realized that maybe Abner wasn't just an amateur politician campaigning for an easy government job. Maybe his fears about the park were well-founded. They all found a news reporter to photograph them, shaking Abner's hand while wishing him the best of luck in keeping all of the visitors safe.

It was a challenge. Day after day, Abner watched as families climbed out of their cars wearing clothes that might have been fine on the streets of whatever city they had journeyed from but were hardly fit for the trails they hoped to traverse. Others came dressed well enough, but clearly, the quality of the outdoor clothes did not match the wearers' experience.

He would meet them as they set out from the parking lot and caution them about the mountain and all the dangers it held. He would remind them that there were rules and reminders posted throughout the park. Ignoring those rules wouldn't result in a ticket or a fine. Ignoring those rules might cost them broken bones or even their life.

Few would have guessed how anxiously this stern and apparently grumpy ranger would await their safe return, counting off every guest until the last adventurer had returned safely for the night. But there were inevitably those who did not return—sometimes a lone hiker, often a whole party. Abner would wait as long as he dared and then start out to search for the missing guests.

He sometimes felt that it was ironic that, although he loved the mountains, he seldom got to walk in them during daylight. Now, he would travel them at night searching and calling out for the lost.

He would search until he found them and then do whatever it took to get them back. Often, they were injured, sometimes severely, and at times, Abner would carry them home. But no matter how much effort he expended, it paled next to the fear that someday he would come too late--that someday he would lose one of his guests forever.

As the park became more popular, it attracted guests from further and further away—more guests who did not understand the dangers hidden in the beauty of the mountains. Abner spent more time searching for and rescuing guests. He knew that his success was one of the things that lured even more visitors to the park. Maybe if he lost someone, the news of their death would underline the warning he faithfully delivered to the visitors. But who would he let go? He would never willingly trade the life of a guest for the most compelling warning.

Then, one day, he had an idea. There was one peak, not the highest, but centrally located, whose summit was visible from almost everywhere in the park. It would be hidden by terrain at times, but almost anywhere in the park, if you journeyed a mile, you would at some point be in view of the summit. Abner began to dream of posting a light atop the summit, which would guide the lost wanderers back to safety. He had no sooner conceived of the idea when he began to lobby for its implementation. He wrote to his boss and suggested the plan.

His supervisor, who had come to trust his ranger, asked him to submit a cost estimate.

Abner had climbed up to the summit on several occasions, but as he climbed up it with an eye to establishing a guiding light, he realized it would be difficult at best. Running electric lines to the mountain's peak would be an enormous job. Getting materials to build a tower to house the light would be almost impossible. The only way to get supplies to the mountain would be to pack them in; no vehicle in the park's motor pool could make the journey.

He wrote to his boss with his findings and wasn't surprised to hear back that there was no funding to attempt such a monumental task. To Abner, no cost could outweigh the lives it might save. Maybe others could calculate the value of life so coldly, but to him, each visitor was a charge committed to him.

He began work on the project himself. The tower was not a big problem. Abner built it with trees that grew on the side of the mountain. He dragged the slender trunks up the ascent and lashed them together to make a light tower.

Through his contacts in the Park System, he was fortunate to meet another ranger who had transferred from the lighthouse service. Navigational lights were increasingly being electrified and automated, and many lightkeeper jobs were being eliminated. The fellow ranger heard about Abner's project and suggested he try to get one of the kerosene lights from a recently electrified lighthouse.

It was just what Abner needed. He carefully carried each part of the lamp to the summit and reassembled it. Most of his work had been done during the off-season, but now, as the busy summer season began, he was ready with his light. The problem was that Abner could not reach the light to extinguish it each morning or reignite it each evening, meaning he had to leave the light constantly burning. At the rate of consumption, this meant that to keep the light burning, he would have to climb to the summit every other day with fuel.

Abner willingly added this to his other responsibilities, but it meant that some days, he wasn't there to meet visitors and explain the significance of the light. He couldn't explain how to use the beacon to find your way home precisely because he was climbing to the summit with fuel to make sure it would stay lit.

Jack, who was growing into a strong boy, saw his father wearing himself out with his trips to the light and his nighttime searches for lost guests who may have ignored the significance of the light or missed Abner's orientation. He didn't resent the demands placed on his father. Instead, he wanted to take his place at his side, helping to carry the burden that sometimes seemed too much for his father.

One day, as his father prepared to make the trip carrying fuel to the summit, Jack came to him dressed in his toughest outdoor clothes and wearing a pair of hand-me-down boots he had from a cousin, which he was likely to grow into within the next few years. "Dad, can I come with you to the peak? I could help carry the kerosene."

It was one of those moments that tests a father. The quickest way to get the job done would be to make the trip himself. Taking Jack would slow him down considerably, and the small amount of kerosene he could carry would not contribute significantly to the effort. On the other hand, if his son aspired to help, he needed to involve him and inspire him. He hoped with all his heart that as Jack grew, he would join him in his vocation of keeping the visitors to the park safe.

Abner accepted Jack's offer. The youngster returned home sweaty, scratched, and thoroughly exhausted but proud of his accomplishment. He would accompany his father every chance he got, and soon, he could match his father's pace on the trail. By the following year, with what Jack carried, they could visit the light every third day. Abner loved the company on the trips and looked forward to the talks they shared.

Then, late one night, while Abner was shepherding a party of lost and disoriented hikers back to their waiting vehicles, he slipped on the trail and turned his ankle. The painful sprain didn't keep him from walking back, but by the time he sought the refuge of his home, Katy found his ankle swollen and bruised. By the next morning, the ankle looked twice its normal size, and Abner could barely hobble with the aid of a crutch.

As he welcomed the visitors, he impressed upon them the dangers of the mountain and painstakingly explained how to use the beacon to find one's way back. By the next night, the light would run out of fuel. The injury that would prevent him from going to the aid of the lost would also prevent him from refilling the light when it was most needed. His only faint hope was that by morning, the foot would be healed enough to make the trip.

After a night of tossing and turning brought on by the pain of his foot and the oddity of not having been on the move all day, Abner finally slumbered deeply as morning arrived. Katy let him sleep. When he finally awoke, it was three hours past his typical start, still early by most people's standard, and in plenty of time to meet the day's visitors. He dressed himself, hobbled to the kitchen, and greeted Katy, struggling not to be cross at her for shutting off the alarm, which he seldom needed but always set.

"Honey, I really needed to be up and try to figure out how to refuel the light."

"You needed the rest. Come and have some breakfast."

"You and Jack can eat, I need to get busy."

"Jack's not here."

"Where is he?"

"I didn't hear him leave, but when I got up, I caught a glimpse of a small figure up on the ridge, so I checked. His pack is gone."

A small ripple of fear passed over Abner. He knew the dangers of the trail to the summit, but it couldn't dim the pride he felt in his son.

When Jack returned, Abner met him as he hung up his pack. The father was wise enough not to shower the boy with praise or gratitude. He shook his hand and asked, "Everything looks shipshape up at the light?"

Jack nodded proudly.

"Well done! Now, let's go meet today's visitors."

Jack made the trip every day until Abner's foot fully healed, and even then, Abner only accompanied him occasionally. Jack had stepped up into a new level of responsibility, and his father didn't want to take it back. His son needed support and encouragement as a young man, not permission to return to boyhood.

The daily trip to the summit had a distinct effect on Jack. The responsibility his father let him keep began to mold his psyche the way that the strenuous effort molded his body. His appetite was impressive, he slept soundly every night, and he carried himself with confidence. When he had free time, he began to look for ways to help his father rather than for ways to amuse himself.

Seeing his son growing before his very eyes, Abner watched for ways to need him more, which is a "flatter-proof" compliment. Then, one night, two different parties failed to return as expected from their outing in the mountains. Abner hurriedly sought out Katie, and as he explained the situation she seemed to understand the decision that faced them. When Abner finished she looked at him and nodded an affirmation of the unasked question. "He's ready."

Abner found Jack preparing for bed and asked him to get dressed and meet him in his office. When the son arrived, his father was contemplating the map covering one wall of the office. "We've got lost guests," he announced. "Two groups. Do you think you can handle a night in the mountains?"

Jack nodded eagerly, "I'd love to come along."

"I'm afraid you won't be coming along. You'll be out alone. I need you to cover the Northern trails. Up along here," he said, pointing to the map. "I'd check this valley and cover the streams around this area. I noticed they had fly rods with them when they set out."

"Here's a pack you can use and a dry cell flashlight you can take. The battery won't last if you use it constantly, so you better save it as much as possible for when you find them. You might have injuries to deal with."

Jack's eyes were shining as he listened to his father. The trust he was being shown was far beyond anything he had expected. He continued to nod as he listened to his father and began packing gear into the pack.

"If you can't bring them back, make them as comfortable as possible and come get me. Hopefully, I'll be back with my group by then." He paused and looked at Jack, held his gaze, and repeated Katie's thought, "You're ready," he declared

Jack was. He brought home the fishermen that night. One had a broken ankle, and the other had fallen to pieces as night and panic had come almost simultaneously. The visitors were amazed and grateful when the young boy stepped out of the night. He kindled a fire, more to build their spirits than for heat, and they warmed themselves while Jack sought out a pair of branches, which he fashioned into a set of crutches. By this time, the uninjured fisherman had begun to collect himself enough to recall some training he had received in an early stint as a boy scout, and with Jack's help, he fashioned a splint for the ankle with materials Jack gathered from the woods.

Slowly, Jack led them homeward until they met Abner coming down the trail to meet them. He said little, but whenever his gaze fell on the small figure leading the cavalcade, he felt immense pride. And Jack could feel it. He had earned the respect of his father and of the men he had rescued. He instinctively knew it was the most valuable thing he could earn.

From then on, Jack participated in almost every search, and he appeared to have a special aptitude for it. Maybe because of his youth, he could approach the park the way a newcomer would. While his father saw the park in terms of the map on his wall, Jack could imagine himself walking a trail for the first time and envision the turns that a visitor might be inclined to take.

He also continued his commitment to the light, making the journey to the summit as needed to keep the beacon shining brightly. Countless people made their way to safety because of that light. They could always count on navigating by its guidance when they lost their way. But there were also many who, despite the light and the warnings, and often because of carelessness or outright foolhardy decisions, found themselves lost in the mountains with night at hand. Their hope was diminishing when Jack appeared to lead them home.

Abner was proud of the record he and his son had compiled; they still had brought everyone back. Some with injuries, even serious ones, but alive. Still, Abner's greatest fear was that someday they would lose their first. When he expressed that fear to his superiors, they assured him that he had no reason to dwell on it. He had done all that could possibly be done to keep visitors safe, far more than they had ever expected. If someday someone ignored his warnings and the light which he provided and went beyond his reach, it was their fault, not his. Abner knew that they were technically right, but this was his park, and the guests were his responsibility. He knew he could never accept a loss so coldly.

Neither would his son. Jack had grown into an amazing young man. He knew the mountains better than Abner himself, and he could run them from the heights to the depths all day long, pack on his back, without even showing signs of tiring. As is so often the case, his confidence seemed to complement a deep and sincere humility.

Frequently, as he brought lost guests to safety, they showered him with praise and offered all sorts of rewards, but none of that turned his head in the least. The simple "well done" he would receive from his father was the only affirmation he seemed to desire.

Some of the rescued guests were serious about wanting to display their gratefulness. Some would report their adventures to the local paper in the town in the valley, often resulting in a story. Jack, who never read the paper, might be given a clipping from a friend of his mother. After reading the story, he would usually toss it in the trash, embarrassed by the exaggerations that the story inevitably contained. Sometimes, a card would come with a gift of money that Jack didn't need. There was nowhere to spend money on the mountain where he loved to spend his time, and it was a point of honor with Abner to provide Jack with everything he needed. The park wouldn't hire him as an employee, but Abner had insisted that any expenses he incurred would come out of the park's budget. The officials back east needed to understand that the hundreds of lives saved came at a cost.

One day, far in the east, two men who had no official connection to the park were diverting themselves on a long train ride with conversation. The two strangers had discussed many things when one mentioned how his life had been saved on a trip into the mountains.

"What a coincidence," the other interrupted, "I almost died one night in a national park, too."

"That's where I was. Funny thing, it was a boy who saved me; he couldn't have been more than twelve or thirteen."

As they compared stories, it became clear that Jack had rescued them both. "You know, that night, I swore I would do something big to express my gratitude. But I somehow never got around to it." admitted one of the men.

"Same here. I wonder how many others like us owe our lives to that kid."

"It would be kind of interesting to find out."

That was the informal beginning of "The Order." The men found it was easier than expected to find others. It seemed like everyone who had visited the park knew of someone who had been rescued. And most of the recipients of Jack's aid were eager to find a way to acknowledge the debt of gratitude they owed. "The Order of Mountainous Gratitude" was formed. They held meetings quarterly, and Jack was always invited. But they were held in distant cities, and the young man didn't want to leave the park guests without his watch-care, so he never made the trip to attend, despite the offer of prepaid train fare and fully funded accommodations.

But even without his presence, the Order grew. Members scoured the local newspaper and contacted individuals whose stories had been featured. They wrote letters to visitors and asked for their recollections of stories. Each clue was followed to its end in an effort to locate all of those whose gratitude could be clearly demonstrated by joining this new club.

The dues and gifts collected by "The Order" were used to tell the story of this remarkable young man who ranged the mountains and had been there in the moment of need for so many lost wanderers. They published a book which became quite popular, not only for visitors who had met Jack, but also for others who read the stories and were filled with admiration for such a hero.

Soon, the leaders of "The Order" were faced with a clamoring by many, who had never even been to the mountains, to be allowed to join the society. The leaders accommodated them by creating an auxiliary membership available for those who hadn't been saved personally but still wanted to belong to "The Order." With these dues, the coffers of "The Order" grew, enabling them to undertake more and more projects to spread the news about Jack and his selfless sacrifice. Which in turn attracted more members and, with them, more dues.

"The Order" had been growing in that manner for half a decade when one of the founders had an inspiration.

Taking the floor at one of the quarterly meetings, he made a suggestion: "Friends, despite all of our efforts to publicize Jack's, he still has never been able to come to one of these meetings. I think we ought to sponsor an event right at the park so that Jack can attend, and we can personally demonstrate to him the depth of our gratitude."

The idea was approved unanimously, and work began immediately on the Gala event. A date was set, and reservations started pouring in. The organizers had contacted Abner and asked to use the headquarters building for the affair, but soon, they contacted him asking if there were any bigger venues available. He offered them the maintenance shed. He could move the park's snowplows and tractors if they wanted to use it. They accepted, and plans moved forward. The small town by the entrance to the park didn't have a catering service, so they hired a service from the nearest city, gladly paying a premium to have someone there to provide a gourmet meal. Money was no object. This was a chance for all those people who had made promises while lost in the mountains to make good their oaths.

To add to the honor, officials from the Park Service, as well as local, state, and federal government figures, were invited to attend the event, which had already received significant publicity.

The maintenance shed had been redecorated to rival a big city ballroom, and a stage had been built for the head table. Buses had been engaged to bring people up the mountain since there wasn't sufficient parking space in the park. Many people arrived early to enjoy the park during the days leading up to the big event. With workers, planners, and visitors all coming and going, the park was the busiest it had ever been. Abner tried not to resent the added chaos because it was intended to honor his son. Still, it sometimes seemed like their chosen expression of gratitude only made the job they were expected to do that much harder. "Oh well," he thought, "it will soon be over."

Jack hardly had time to think about the event; he was so busy keeping the increased number of visitors safe on the mountain trails.

Finally, the night of the event arrived. The maintenance shed/banquet hall was filling with people, and the smell of delicious food was wafting out of the building that had been remodeled into a temporary kitchen. VIPs began arriving, along with the founders of "The Order." They mingled with the guests and enjoyed the appetizers being circulated by the professional wait staff brought in for the night.

Except for the head table, the seating was on a first-come, first-serve basis. Even though it was still a while before the meal was scheduled to start, guest began hovering around their prospective seats, staking a claim to the good seats close to the stage. Never before had so much finery been seen this far up the mountain. Guests were wearing their very best clothes in honor of their hero. Tuxedos and evening gowns, marked the wealthiest of the guests while others of more modest means made sure they wore the best they could afford.

Even the organizers had to admit surprise at the turnout for the evening. It would be a real tribute to someone who certainly deserved it. They could imagine how honored the young man would be when he arrived.

The problem was that no one could find Jack. The caterer was getting concerned, knowing that the quality of the food would diminish if the meal was delayed, but the organizers insisted that they couldn't start the meal without the guest of honor. The guests were getting restless, and as people got tired of hovering around their coveted seats close to the stage, they would wander away only to find their coveted seats quickly claimed by others. Some relinquished their positions reluctantly, while others sought out the organizers requesting a policy about saving seats. But the organizers were too busy trying to pacify the head caterer, who was sure the meal would be wrecked if they waited longer. The appetizers had been finished long ago, and people were growing hungry.

Finally, someone found out why there was a wait. A family who had gone out onto the mountain for the day had not returned when expected, and Jack had gone out to find them.

The crowd began to polarize. One contingent was sure that the last thing a thoughtful young man like Jack would want was to keep a crowd of hungry people waiting. They were in favor of starting the meal. Another contingent thought that a meal to honor Jack should be willing to wait for his return. The chef thought only about how his masterpiece was being ruined by the self-centeredness of the guest of honor. Others were more understanding and argued that since they all had been in the same situation, they could hardly begrudge Jack his journey onto the mountain to save other lost people.

Only six people got up from their seats and quietly made their way out of the hall. They found their way up to the ranger's house and asked Katy if they could help. Lacking enough battery lights for everyone, she offered some lanterns and dug up several old pairs of shoes for some who needed more rugged footwear. She assigned them sectors of the park to search and reminded them how to navigate from the beacon.

The factions in the banquet hall became more pronounced, and the chef walked out, saying he wanted to be far away when the meal was served. It was wrecked, and he wanted it clear that it wasn't his fault. The faction in favor of eating right away grew as hunger became a bigger issue. The organizers were almost ready to give in when a rumor spread through the hall that the lost family had been found.

It still seemed to take forever for Jack and his father to come to the hall. They were welcomed by the assembled crowd, and seeing them in their sturdy outdoor clothes somehow seemed appropriate despite the finery around them. These were men of the mountains who made it their business to save the lost. They were seated at the head table, and the various dignitaries began abbreviated versions of their speeches.

While the program went on, a small group of a half dozen people came into the hall. They looked around and found that almost all the seats had been filled. The head waiter immediately recognized another problem on this disastrous night. These late arrivals were in no way dressed for the banquet. Their clothes were dirty and torn, and several of the people had clunky boots on, which matched the condition of their clothes but not the style. It was as if they had put on their best clothes and then worn them to work for a week.

The head waiter didn't know whether he dared send them away, but at least he could get them a table away from the rest of the crowd. He hurried over and offered to set up a table for them before they started making their way to the various empty seats among the better-dressed guests.

Two shaky card tables were found and quickly set with whatever dishes could be found.

Meanwhile, the speeches were wrapping up on the stage, and it was finally time to serve the meal. The final act of honor planned for the evening was the serving of the head table. Two key organizers, a mayor and a state legislator, were scheduled to serve Jack. The men went to join the procession, which would bring the guest of honor his supper and start the long-awaited meal. The last speaker finished his brief message and called for a round of applause for their hero. Jack rose from his seat and looked out at the crowd. The applause diminished, and the hall fell silent. The crowd waited breathlessly for their hero to speak.

At first, they thought he was speechless, overawed by the crowd's gratitude. But as they watched, it seemed more like he was looking for someone in particular in the crowded hall. Finally, he fixed his eyes on the two decrepit card tables. He motioned to the men carrying the food for the head table to follow him, wound his way through the crowd, and sat down with the tattered guests who had joined him on the search.

Think for a minute.
Which group does your
expression of gratitude resemble?
Have noble aims, demanding your tireless effort
clouded the reality that
"the Son of man came to seek
and to save that which was lost."

Is it time for you to leave the banquet
to search the wilderness?
You may find a fellowship on the mountain
you have never felt at the table.

"We are children of God: and if children, then heirs;
heirs of God and joint heirs with Christ;
If it so be that we suffer with him...."

-Paul